Vital Signs

Jamaica Layne

Vital Signs

Ravenous Romance™
100 Cummings Center
Suite 123A
Beverly, MA 01915

A version of this work was previously published in electronic form by Ravenous Romance.

ISBN-13-978-1-60777-644-4

Chapter One

"YOU'LL BE working another double-shift tonight," Joanna Watson's boss growled at her from the other side of the nurse's station. "Lindsay's still out with the flu, plus the new chief surgeon is pulling *triple* time in the operating room—triple, as in working twenty-four hours *straight*. And we've only got half the nurses we need on staff as it is."

Joanna Watson knitted her perfectly arched strawberry-blond brows together. "Damn it," she muttered. Yet another sleepless night in the OR was the last thing she needed.

What Joanna needed more than anything right now was a nap.

"Joanna? Did you hear what I just said?" Maryam Malone, Covington Community Hospital's Surgery and Recovery department's sixty-something head nurse, tapped Joanna on the shoulder with a ballpoint pen that advertised the newest erectile-dysfunction drug. Maryam had a whole collection of erectile-dysfunction drug pens— she accumulated them on her desk as a homage to her late husband, who had died of a heart attack last year immediately following a Viagra-fueled marathon lovemaking session. Joanna had to shake her head rapidly to clear it of all the sexually suggestive brand names (Levitra, Viagra, Cialis) the pen triggered in her weary brain.

"Joanna?" Maryam asked. "Are you all right?"

"Yes, I am. I'm sorry—I guess I'm just a little irritated is all."

"Why?"

"I worked my butt off for Dr. Turnblatt for three straight months before he retired. I *earned* this time off from the OR, Maryam. Joe Middleton promised it to me. And now you're expecting me to go right back in there, without even a *single day* off? It's not fair!"

"Well, *life's* not fair, sweetie," Maryam clucked. "But don't worry. Given the situation, I got good old Mr. Middleton to approve double-overtime pay for you instead of the usual time-and-a-half. That's the best I can do until Lindsay gets over the flu. Oh, and I should warn you. The new guy is a real jerk. Dr. Wilkinson is a taskmaster, an S.O.B, and an evil criminal mastermind all rolled into one."

Joanna chuckled and finished signing off on some medical supply requisitions. "I'm sure he's not as bad as all that."

Maryam laughed. "That's easy for you to say. You haven't met him yet. I've been dealing with him for the past three days, and I've got to tell you, Joanna, the guy's got about as much charisma as Darth Vader on crack."

Joanna started grinding her teeth. A raging, supermacho surgeon making her life miserable in the OR was the last thing she needed after the hellish three months she'd just spent stroking Dr. Turnblatt's (thankfully) now-retired ego. As if that weren't bad enough, her divorce had just been made final a month prior to that.

A divorce that was a long time in coming. She'd spent almost three years legally separated from her petty ex-husband while they bickered in court over their marital assets. In the end, most of the marital assets went to pay legal bills, leaving Joanna with little besides the equity in her modest condo, her nursing job, and what little was left of her dignity.

"All right," Joanna finally sighed, surrendering to her fate. "I'll consider myself forewarned. I'll take the shift on one condition."

Maryam's nostrils flared. "What's that?"

"Give me half an hour to take a nap, and another half-hour to get some dinner. I'll just go down to the cafeteria lounge for a sandwich or something. I won't be long."

"All right, deal. But hurry up about it."

Joanna sighed, finished filing her paperwork, and started down the hall towards the elevators.

Joanna's sturdy nursing shoes squeaked on the linoleum. *Viagra. Cialis. Levitra. Levitra. Viagra. Cialis.* Brand names from dozens of commercials featuring ridiculously sexy middle-aged men rang out in her brain like church bells with every step she took. Why couldn't she get all those annoying drugs out of her mind? It's not like she would ever need to take them herself. It's not like anyone had taken them for the purpose of satisfying *her*, either. She'd had no sex life to speak of for the past three years.

She'd had no sex life to speak of long before her divorce was even a consideration, in fact. Even during their ten-year marriage, Bob (her dull bean-counter of an ex-husband) had always been too proud to admit that he was exactly the kind of man the drug companies had in mind when they invented Viagra. Bob had spent more of their marriage trying in vain to get his dick up than he had doing anything else.

Joanna shook her head hard, trying to clear it of the painful memories. But try as she might, she just couldn't get sex off her mind. *What's wrong with me*? she thought. *It's probably just the exhaustion. Either that or I've been watching too many Viagra commericals.*

Joanna headed for the elevators. She'd catch a ride to the lower-level cafeteria on one of them, grab a sandwich and a coffee for two bucks, and hopefully grab a quick nap in the nurse's lounge before reporting for duty in the dreaded Dr. Harlan Wilkinson's operating room. Joanna wasn't nervous or apprehensive at meeting the newest S.O.B.-surgeon on the block—she'd met dozens of aggressive, Type-A physicians in her career—she was just annoyed. Annoyed, and damn tired. A nice, quiet break was all she needed.

A nice, quiet break, that's all.

But a nice, quiet break wasn't exactly what was in store for her. Not by a long shot.

Chapter Two

JOANNA STEPPED into the elevator when it arrived on her floor. She pressed the "DOOR CLOSE" button several times, trying in vain to get the elevator moving. But the old contraption, designed in the 1950s for ferrying slow-moving gurneys and wheelchairs, wasn't cooperating.

"Damn it," she mumbled under her breath, mashing the "DOOR CLOSE" button again. At last, the squeaky car doors began to shut.

"HOLD THAT GODDAMN THING! HOLD IT!" A booming male voice echoed into the elevator car from somewhere down the hall. A deep, gravelly, slightly hoarse male voice.

A voice that for some unknown reason, gave Joanna pause.

Her finger floated involuntarily to the "DOOR OPEN" button. She almost didn't notice it happening until the last possible second, when the doors were nearly shut.

"DID YOU HEAR ME?" the voice thundered. "*Hold* it!"

Joanna pressed the "DOOR OPEN" button without exactly knowing why. She wanted nothing more than to get to the basement for her coffee break, but something in the unseen man's voice made her waver.

The elevator doors glided open again. A tall, scowling man stood on the other side of them.

A tall, scowling, rumpled, sweaty, and very *attractive* man. A man that Joanna hadn't seen before. A man wearing dirty scrubs, a vicious frown, and at least three-days' growth of stubby beard that did nothing to deter from his natural good looks.

"Are you hard of hearing?" the man growled at her. "I asked you to *hold* this goddamn elevator."

Joanna didn't respond for nearly thirty seconds. She set her jaw and returned the man's steely, aquamarine-eyed gaze. As a seasoned hospital nurse, she was accustomed to difficult, short-tempered people. She was used to rude, crude, obnoxious behavior by both patients *and* doctors. What she was *not* used to was that rude, crude behavior emanating from a man who was so ruggedly handsome that it made the pit of her stomach quaver.

"Sorry, I thought I *was* holding it for you," was Joanna's curt reply.

The scowling man blinked twice. He held the elevator doors open with his hands. Joanna noticed that unlike the rest of his unkempt, rugged self, both his hands were immaculately manicured, the skin moisturized, the fingers long and nimble. She'd seen hands like that often enough to know exactly what they were used for.

They were a surgeon's hands.

Joanna stepped to the rear of the elevator and leaned against its cool stainless-steel wall. The scowling surgeon stepped inside the car without another word. He stared straight ahead, and did nothing more to acknowledge Joanna's presence.

Joanna gazed at their reflection in the elevator's mirrored doors as the car jerked and vibrated its way down towards the hospital basement. The scowling surgeon's jaw tensed in a series of nervous tics. His feet shuffled back and forth on the metal floor of the elevator car. He checked his watch.

"Goddamn it, this has got to be the slowest fucking elevator in the entire state of North Carolina," he hissed just as the elevator car lurched to a sudden stop that sent Joanna tumbling to the floor. The man lost his balance for the slightest moment, but then righted himself against the wall. He stared down at Joanna on the floor, but said nothing.

It took her a moment to collect her wits from the fall, but she soon gathered her composure and stared back up at this man, who had to be one of the rudest of all the rude surgeons that she'd ever encountered in her fifteen years as a nurse. She knew his type, all right. He was acid, Type-A, abrasive-S.O.B.-surgeon all the way. Since she hadn't seen him anywhere around before, Joanna hoped against hope that Mr. Personality here was one of the hospital's out-patient surgeons—the ones who did run-of-the-mill tummy tucks for the local socialites and stomach stapling jobs for the hopelessly obese—instead of the heavy-duty inpatient procedures she usually assisted on. God knew she didn't want to get stuck in the OR with this chump. Whoever this man was, he obviously didn't belong in her department. He was probably just lost.

At least, she *hoped* he was lost.

Joanna rubbed her bruised tailbone. As a proper North Carolina lady, Joanna expected to be treated with a certain level of courtesy from men. "Aren't you going to help me up, Doctor?"

Mr. Personality frowned down at her. "Why? You don't look in-jured to me."

"Some would call it gentlemanly courtesy to help a lady up after she falls."

He scoffed. "Not where I come from. Where I come from, it's every man for himself."

Offended, Joanna bit her tongue, and pulled herself upright without comment.

"Goddamn it," Mr. Personality said again as he banged on the elevator doors. Joanna noticed the hint of a Northern city accent. She couldn't place which one—New York, or maybe Boston. "Looks like this goddamn thing is stuck."

Joanna sighed and rolled her eyes. "It certainly looks that way, sir. Too bad I'm stuck in here with you." She tried to make her voice sound as nasty as his, but her rolling, native-Carolina accent just made her insult seem overly polite.

"I'll just forget I heard that," Mr. Personality seethed just as his beeper went off. He pulled it off his waistband, read the return phone number, and exclaimed, "Fuck!"

"I'd appreciate it if you watch your language, Doctor," Joanna said, her voice tight and even. "This is a hospital, not a roadside bar."

"Pardon me, miss, but I'll swear as much as I fucking feel like swearing when I'm stuck in a goddamn elevator. I'm getting paged by the trauma team and I can't return the page because I'm stuck in here without a phone."

Joanna reached into the left pocket of her scrubs and pulled out a cell phone, which she handed to Mr. Personality. He snatched it out of her hands without a word.

"You're welcome," she hissed. He ignored her and dialed the phone.

Joanna folded her arms and glared at Mr. Personality while he waited for someone in Trauma to answer his call. After a moment, someone did.

"Yeah, this is Dr. Harlan Wilkinson here, returning a page?"

Joanna felt all the blood drain from her face. Dr. Harlan Wilkinson? Mr. Personality was *Dr. Harlan Wilkinson?*

As in, the hospital's new head of surgery?

Oh, shit.

"Sorry, I can't get down there right now," Dr. Wilkinson barked into her phone. "I'm stuck in the goddamn elevator with some idiot nurse."

At this, Joanna gritted her teeth and shot Dr. Wilkinson the most vicious look she could manage. He stared back, then looked her up and down. She felt her skin prickle under his gaze.

"Yeah, well, you'll just have to have one of the residents handle it until I can get out of this tin can," Dr. Wilkinson shouted into the phone. "Send the goddamn maintenance people up here to get me out of this thing, why don't you?"

Dr. Wilkinson snapped Joanna's cell phone shut and passed it back to her as if it were contaminated with flesh-eating bacteria. She slipped it back into the hip pocket of her scrubs. As she did, she noticed that for some strange reason, her groin had started to feel a little warm.

"For your information, Dr. Wilkinson, I am not an idiot," Joanna heard herself say.

Dr. Wilkinson raised his eyebrows, but didn't respond.

"I am a trained, highly experienced nurse. A *surgical* nurse."

Dr. Wilkinson's eyebrows lowered. Joanna noticed he had a deep furrow between them, a furrow that she couldn't help staring at. "Oh?" he asked.

"I have been assigned to assist you in your surgical procedures this evening," she retorted. "*After* I've had my coffee break, that is."

Dr. Wilkinson absently rubbed at the stubble on his chin. "You can forget about that," he muttered. "I don't believe in coffee breaks."

Joanna did a double-take. "I'll have you know that I am fully entitled to take this break. I've been working double shifts every day for the past three weeks without a single day off. I've already worked an eight-hour shift today in Recovery straight through without a lunch hour, plus Head Nurse Malone authorized it since I wasn't even supposed to be working second shift at all today—"

"You don't work for Head Nurse Malone," Dr. Wilkinson said matter-of-factly.

The *nerve* of this guy, telling her who she did and did not work for! She'd teach Mr. Personality here a thing or two. Joanna unfolded her arms and stamped her foot. "Yes, I do. She's the head nurse in my department, and—"

"You work for me. *Only* for me. You're Joanna Watson, aren't you?"

Joanna blinked. "How did you know?"

A slow smile spread across Dr. Wilkinson's stubbled face. "I just read your ID badge."

Joanna felt her cheeks flush with embarrassment. "Oh. Right."

"When the hospital hired me to take over for Dr. Turnblatt, one of the terms I worked into my contract was that I'd be guaranteed to have the best surgical nurses on staff here at my disposal whenever I wanted them, day or night—and that I'd have absolute control over their scheduling and assignments. And my sources tell me that the best surgical nurse on staff here at Covington Community Hospital is, hands down, Joanna Watson. Apparently, that's you."

At this, Joanna was flattered, but she wasn't about to show it. Not to Mr. Personality here. She couldn't allow him that satisfaction.

"That doesn't mean I *work* for you. I report to the head nurse, *not* to you—"

"You do now. You'll be getting a memo on that sometime tomorrow. Per the terms of my contract, you belong to me."

Joanna's jaw dropped into her chin with a painful *thud*. "But—"

Dr. Wilkinson put up his well-manicured hand to cut her off. "I need you for my next scheduled surgery. That's in thirty minutes. It's a trauma case, a twenty-year-old college kid with a very nasty compound femur fracture he got jumping off the roof of his frat house over at Hunton College. I'm doing it myself because the nearest orthopaedist is two hours away in Durham. It'll take a good couple hours of OR time to stabilize this kid, since he's already lost a lot of blood, and has alcohol poisoning to boot. As soon as maintenance gets us out of this goddamn elevator, Watson, I am going down to the ER to assess this case, and while I am doing that, you are to report straight back up to the Surgery floor to scrub up for the job. You belong to *me* for the rest of your shift, and you'll do what *I* say. Got it?"

Joanna sucked in a deep, heavy breath and blew it out. It was all she could do to keep herself from throttling him. What a bastard.

She finally lowered her gaze to the floor of the elevator and gave the doctor a single nod.

"Good."

Joanna summoned the courage to look Dr Wilkinson straight in the eye—and as she did, she felt her crotch go even warmer. "So, what do we do if they can't get us out of the elevator?" she asked.

Dr. Wilkinson shrugged. "Well, then I suppose we'd be screwed," he said, then looked Joanna up and down once more. "I've gotta be honest, Ms. Watson. You aren't exactly how I pictured you when the administration described your qualifications."

Joanna raised one eyebrow. "And how, pray tell, *did* you picture me?"

Dr. Wilkinson looked Joanna up and down yet again—slower this time. "I pictured you as middle-aged, frumpy, overweight, and with a blue-dyed beehive hairdo."

Joanna laughed. "You just described my boss, Maryam Malone."

A slow smile tugged at one corner of the surgeon's mouth. "Well, that's amusing," he said. "Though in my experience, most good OR nurses look just like that. I haven't run into a decent OR nurse under the age of forty-five in, well, never. Let alone one as young and attractive as you are."

Joanna blushed to her eardrums. "Well, thank you for the compliment," she said. "At least I *think* it's a compliment. For all I know, you're insulting me for not having enough experience."

"I doubt you'd have such a stellar reputation if you lacked experience," the surgeon replied, his eyes sparkling. "Though you don't exactly look like someone who's tough enough to work for twenty-four hours straight on your feet in the OR." He looked up and down her body again, and this time, every pore of Joanna's skin felt as if he were caressing it under his gaze. "You're awfully petite for OR work, Watson. And you look pretty damn good for someone who claims to be overworked and exhausted." Dr. Wilkinson shifted his weight, leaned back against the elevator's cold steel wall. "Hell, if this is how you look on a bad day, I'd love to catch you on a good one sometime."

Joanna's breath caught. Was this man coming on to her? It certainly seemed that way.

Several awkward minutes passed. There was a harsh, metallic grinding noise from somewhere high above. The elevator jerked sharply again, then dropped further and stopped short, sending Joanna toppling forward into Dr. Wilkinson's arms.

Then the lights went out.

They weren't getting out of there anytime soon, that was obvious. Dr. Wilkinson took it as his cue to hold Joanna even tighter.

The feel of Dr. Wilkinson's firm-yet-tender grip on her body sent Joanna reeling. Now, her entire lower half was on fire. She could hear heavy breathing somewhere in the darkness—and she was shocked when she realized it was her own.

"Well, now it really looks like we're screwed," Dr. Wilkinson said through the darkness, his voice suddenly deeper. "I hope that poor frat boy doesn't bleed to death because of this." He didn't let go of Joanna, as she expected he would. Instead, he just pulled her even closer.

"I'm sure the Trauma people will stabilize him until we can get out of here," she replied, breathless.

"What do you propose we do in the meantime, Joanna?" Dr. Wilkinson said, using her given name for the first time. "Because it looks like we could be stuck in here for quite a while."

"I—" was all Joanna could muster before Dr. Wilkinson's mouth closed upon hers. They kissed for almost a full minute, their tongues doing a wild, wet tango until Joanna finally had to come up for air.

"What the hell was that for?" she stammered.

"You'll have to forgive me," Dr. Wilkinson said. "Sometimes I have a tendency to come on a little strong."

"I'll say." The proper, refined Southern lady in Joanna was mortified and offended at what had just happened. But the raw, repressed, sex-hungry woman she was inside wanted things to keep progressing just as they were. Joanna had had sex on the brain for days, and now, here it was just inches away from her. She'd be crazy not to take advantage of it—even if it would be with her new boss. Still—

"It's all right, Joanna," Dr. Wilkinson said, caressing the side of her face. "No one will ever know. It'll be our little secret."

"Dr. Wilkinson—"

He held a finger to her lips. "Hush," he said. "And as long as we're stuck in here together, you can call me Harlan."

Joanna could tell just how aroused Harlan was when he pulled her closer. The bulge at his crotch was unmistakable.

Either he was glad to see her, or that was a nuclear warhead in his pocket.

And Joanna wasn't exactly a cold fish at the moment, either. Her panties were damp. She hadn't made love in more than three years. She was obsessed with Viagra commercials. Even if it went against all her principles as a properly raised Southern lady, Joanna would be lying through her teeth if she said she didn't want to get down and dirty with her arrogant-S.O.B.-surgeon-slash-boss right here, right now.

"All right, Harlan," she said, her voice husky with desire. "Let's do it. As long as what happens here, stays here."

"What happens here, stays here," Harlan repeated. "Now you're talking."

Before Joanna even knew what was happening, half her clothes were on the floor and Harlan was inside her.

They made love pressed up against the stainless-steel wall of the elevator for almost twenty minutes, their heavy breathing and the sounds and sighs of their joining the only sounds in the pitch darkness. They each reached their climax at the same time, an incredible interstellar explosion that rocketed off the steel walls.

Joanna collapsed against Harlan's shoulder. "Thank you," she whispered. "Thank you so much."

"You're welcome," he whispered back, gently nuzzling her ear. "I hope it was good for you."

"It was better than good," Joanna sighed. "It was the best I ever had."

As if on cue, the elevator lights flashed back on, and the elevator suddenly lurched back into motion. Joanna and Harlan barely had enough time to disentangle themselves and dress before the elevator car landed on the first floor, just steps away from the trauma center.

Dr. Wilkinson stepped out of the elevator, then paused to turn around, holding open the battered doors with one immaculate hand. In an instant, every shred of the ardent lover Joanna had come to know in the darkness was gone, replaced by the hard-edged surgeon she'd first met almost a half-hour before. "I'll see you upstairs in a few minutes," Harlan said, his voice curt and businesslike. "Be scrubbed, masked and ready to go by the time I get up there. And don't be late. If you are, I'll write you up."

Write her up?

What the hell?

"But—" Joanna stammered. "What about—"

Dr. Wilkinson pointed inside the elevator with his free hand. "What happens here, stays here," he said. "As we agreed. Good-bye, Watson."

Nurse Malone had been far too kind in her description of Dr. Wilkinson. "Darth Vader on crack" was no way to describe him. The man was Ivan the Terrible, Joseph Stalin, and Attila the Hun all rolled into one.

As the elevator doors slid shut, it was all Joanna could do to keep from pounding her fists against them in rage.

Chapter Three

SHIRLEY DANIELS was totally fed up with Covington Community Hospital.

She'd been slaving away as a certified nurse-anesthetist there for years, working double shifts six days a week for less than half what she could earn working at a big research hospital in Raleigh-Durham or Charlotte. As if that weren't bad enough, now she had to anesthetize patients in the OR for that rat bastard Dr. Harlan Wilkinson, who apparently flew down to North Carolina from his hoity-toity research hospital in Boston for the sole purpose of making her and everyone she worked with miserable.

Not only did the rude, crude Yankee make no secret of the fact he thought nurses had no business administering anesthesia, he had absolutely no respect for common courtesy. He swore like a sailor in the OR, called her "Daniels" (as if she were a grunt in the U.S. Army instead of a well-educated Southern lady) and even insisted that Shirley play heavy-metal CDs in the OR sound system instead of the light easy-listening tunes she preferred—because, as Dr. Wilkinson put it, "the patient's already asleep, Daniels. The rest of us don't need to join him in Dreamland because of your sappy choice in music."

What an asshole.

And yet, the aggressive Yankee surgeon stirred feelings in Shirley's mind and body she hadn't felt in a long, long time. When she walked out of the OR ten minutes ago, her head was throbbing and her throat smarting with anger and offense.

But her crotch was on fire.

Shirley stood under the lukewarm shower in the nurses' locker room and ground her teeth. She couldn't work under these conditions. She decided it was high time to start looking for another job.

But where? She couldn't leave Statesville—not as long as her mother and father both remained ill and frail in a nearby nursing home. Her family obligations had kept her in this godforsaken town for way longer than she'd ever planned, but there just wasn't anything she could do about it now. Shirley was all her parents had in the world—and they needed her close by. As much as Shirley wanted to get away, there was no way she could leave Statesville until both her mother and father were dead. And that could take years.

In the meantime, Shirley could only watch helplessly as her youth and her chances at romance and a family of her own slipped away further and further with every passing year. Shirley might be a hardworking, stiff-upper-lip nurse who put the needs of her family above her own—but she wasn't dead, either. She had needs, damn it. Needs that just weren't being met.

Needs that seemed to become more pronounced whenever she was in the same room with Dr. Harlan Wilkinson.

Shirley pushed the faucet all the way over to "COLD" and stood under the icy shower stream, hoping the frigid water would chill things out down south.

It didn't. Her crotch was still on fire. Something had to give, and fast.

Dr. Harlan Wilkinson was definitely an asshole. But he was also an aphrodisiac.

Shirley's love life had been so dormant for so long, the sensual part of her was almost dead and buried. And if Dr. Wilkinson hadn't perked Shirley up in the crotch department upon his arrival, Shirley would probably have qualified for born-again virgin status.

But that was then, this is now, Shirley thought to herself. *Now, I'm a different woman.*

But all the time in the world couldn't bring back all the frigid, barren years she'd lost. She'd frittered away her youth working double hospital shifts and caring for her aged parents—years she could have spent partying, dating, and having lots of hot casual sex, like all her sorority sisters from college had. It didn't seem fair.

Still, Shirley was only thirty-four. She was in good shape from pulling so many long, hard shifts in the OR. She still had a good complexion, and long, shiny brown hair that she conditioned with a homemade lemon-and-mayonnaise concoction every Sunday night. And her deep violet-blue eyes—by far her best feature—were arresting. Or they were when she wasn't completely exhausted from too many double shifts in the OR, anyway. There was no reason she couldn't attract a man. Even at her most ragged, she was an attractive woman, damn it.

Hell, if she could manage to get a facial, a new haircut and a couple of days off, Shirley Daniels could even be hot.

Shirley rinsed off, turned off the tap, and grabbed her towel from its hook just outside her shower stall. As she toweled off her now-buzzing body, Shirley decided it was high time to turn over a new leaf—where romance was concerned, anyway. Sure, she still had to work ungodly hours in the OR in order to keep her job and keep a nursing-home roof over her parents' heads. But that didn't mean she couldn't have a love life. The arrival of the sexy Yankee with the cocky attitude—unattainable as he might be—had inspired Shirley to look for sensuality in new and unlikely places.

Shirley Daniels had entered a new phase in life. Something new and exciting was definitely on the horizon. The only question was: when would it happen? And who would her partner (or partners) be?

Only time would tell.

Chapter Four

IN ALL her nursing career, Joanna Watson had never once wished to trade places with the person on the operating table. But she supposed there was a first time for everything. Because at that moment, Joanna would have given anything to trade places with Jonah Jones, the twenty-year-old college student who lay unconscious on the operating table with pieces of his femur sticking out of his leg in three separate places. At least *he* was enjoying some peace and quiet underneath all that anesthesia.

Unlike Joanna.

"THIS IS NOT THE RETRACTOR I ASKED FOR!" Dr. Wilkinson boomed at her, loud enough to wake up all the patients in Recovery next door.

"Yes, it is, Dr. Wilkinson," she replied coolly. "You asked for the eight-centimeter. That's exactly what I gave you."

"Watson, I thought you were supposed to be the best surgical nurse on staff here," Mr. Personality growled. "If that were true, then you would know that I didn't *mean* the eight-centimeter, I meant the *eighteen*-centimeter. Any idiot could see that an eight-centimeter is too small for the area I'm working on right now."

"Any idiot could ask for the right size retractor, too," Joanna seethed, handing him the correct one.

Joanna glanced over at Shirley Daniels, the petite nurse-anesthe-tist on this operation, and noticed that the woman was red in the face. A fine sheen of perspiration stood out on her forehead, and she was breathing heavily. "Is the patient showing any sign of aware-ness, doctor?" Shirley stammered in a deep, husky voice not at all like her usual businesslike tone in the OR.

For a moment, Joanna thought the woman sounded really turned on—almost like someone you'd hear on a phone sex line. But then Joanna thought better of it. She was probably just imagining things. After all, Shirley Daniels wasn't exactly known around town for having a social life, let alone as someone who got sexed up in the OR. But still—

"I'm sure the patient will let us know if he wakes up, damn it." Dr. Wilkinson's harsh Yankee growl broke Joanna out of her reverie. She flinched, but out of the corner of her eye, Joanna thought she could see the corners of Shirley's eyes pointing upward behind her mask—that and the sex flush fast showing itself on her forehead in-dicated the usually reserved, uptight woman was feeling naughty.

Shirley Daniels was getting off on Dr. Wilkinson's rude remarks. And Joanna didn't like it one bit.

What the hell was going on?

Joanna felt a sharp jab of jealousy in her belly. She shook her head violently back and forth, trying to clear it of any and all sexual thoughts. She couldn't lose her concentration in the OR over a petty romantic rivalry with another nurse. A patient's life was at stake, after all. And it wasn't as if Joanna really had much of a claim on Dr. Wilkinson anyway. One casual screw in an elevator didn't exactly add up to a romantic relationship.

"Where the hell's the hook scissors I asked you for five minutes ago, Watson?" Dr. Wilkinson snarled as he manipulated one of poor Jonah Jones's broken femur ends back into place. "Are you day-dreaming, or what?"

"You never asked me for any hook scissors, Doctor." Joanna ground her teeth behind her paper mask again, and felt her own cheeks grow hot. "But perhaps you were just *thinking* about how you needed them five minutes ago and assumed I had read your mind." Joanna took care to hold her Carolina twang in check, and this time she actually managed to sound a little mean.

Her change in tone seemed to have worked. Dr. Wilkinson's eyes widened slightly underneath the clear plastic face screen that protected his eyes from blood and debris. Although his paper surgical mask covered most of his features, Joanna could tell from the pinching corners of his deep-blue eyes that he was smiling a little. "A good nurse is *always* capable of reading a surgeon's mind, Watson," he said. "Isn't that right, Daniels?"

"Oh *yes*, Doctor," Shirley replied, her voice deep and sultry. Now there was no mistaking what that woman had on her mind.

Joanna bit her lip as she felt her crotch heating up. The whole situation was getting ridiculous. She suddenly felt as if she were working on the set of *Grey's Anatomy* instead of a conservative, underfunded rural hospital where sex was always the last possible thing on anyone's mind.

Her hand hovered over the sterile surgical tool tray. "Was it the number six hook scissors you wanted, Doctor, or the number eight?"

"Eight," Dr. Wilkinson replied as he took the scissors from her and used them to clip off the thread he was using to stitch a broken blood vessel. When he was finished, he handed them back to Joanna. When the scissors landed in her palm, Dr. Wilkinson's ice-blue eyes met hers. "Thank you," he said, his voice much calmer and gentler than before.

She'd tamed the man a bit.

Touché, Joanna.

"I'll be ready to insert the first rod in just a minute," he said. "Do you have it ready?"

"Yes, Doctor, it's right here. Already sterile."

"What about the Steinmann pins?" Dr. Wilkinson was still staring straight into Joanna's eyes. It made her uneasy, but she stared straight back, hard and without blinking. The same stomach quavering she'd felt back in the elevator returned suddenly, startling her so much she almost upset the surgical tool tray.

"Watson?" Dr. Wilkinson barked, his voice taking on its familiar angry edge again. "I asked you a question."

Joanna broke off her return stare and shook her head rapidly to regain her composure. "S-sorry. The Steinmann pins are also here and ready. I have twelve of them—the nine you asked for, plus three extra, just in case."

Dr. Wilkinson did a double-take. "Just in case of what?"

Joanna sucked in her breath again before answering. "Just in case you break one," she said. "It's been known to happen."

Dr. Wilkinson scoffed. "Ha. Not on my watch." All sign of the calmer, gentler self he'd revealed moments ago were gone. "I've never broken a pin in my entire goddamn career, and I don't expect to start now."

McDreamy the man definitely was not.

So much for being transplanted onto the *Grey's Anatomy* set.

Joanna bit her tongue to keep from laughing. Obviously Mr. Personality here thought he was incapable of ever making a mistake in the OR, even such a common one as breaking a Steinmann pin while inserting it into a broken femur bone. Steinmann pins often snapped the first time a surgeon tried to insert them into a young person's strong bones—they were originally designed for mending the brittle bones of the elderly, not the rock-hard, solid ones of drunken frat boys who had fallen from three stories.

Dr. Wilkinson aligned the two remaining sections of femur into something sort of resembling a normal leg. "Now it's time to place the external fixator. Watson, please hand me the Wagner device."

Joanna took up the heavy, metal-and-plastic Wagner device. Joanna knew that the proper way to apply an external fixator on a femur break was to wait until *after* the rods and Steinmann pins were inserted, stabilized, and most of the incision stitched up—not the other way around, as it appeared Dr. Wilkinson wanted to do. She hesitated.

"Watson, I asked you to hand me the damn Wagner device."

"No."

Dr. Wilkinson dropped his scalpel. It clattered to the tiled operating room floor. "Excuse me?"

"I said, *no*, Doctor."

Dr. Wilkinson snatched the unwieldy thing right out of Joanna's hands. "You want to change that answer, Watson?"

"No, Doctor, I don't. I feel it is my duty to inform you that usual procedure on femur repair operations is to insert the Steinmann pins, rods, and intermedullary screws *before* you apply external fixation." Joanna had to force these words from her lips. She had broken out into a cold sweat. It was all she could do to keep from fainting as she prepared herself for Dr. Wilkinson's surely coming verbal assault. Still, even as she shivered in fear, her crotch temperature reached a boiling point.

Dr. Wilkinson's glacial eyes bore into her. "Just who exactly is the surgeon in here, Watson?"

"With all due respect, Doctor, I assisted Army orthopaedists on several femur repair operations on young men like this when I was working at Walter Reed. A lot of kids coming back from Desert Storm broke their femurs falling off tanks and jumping out of planes. So I am more than familiar with standard procedure on surgeries like this." Joanna set her jaw, fully expecting to be sworn at.

Dr. Wilkinson's grip on the Wagner device loosened. In a move that stunned both Joanna and Shirley, he walked over to Joanna's side of the operating table and replaced the device on its tray, then stepped back over to the spot where he'd been working. The two nurses watched his every move, breathless.

The surgeon's icy gaze locked with Joanna's bright green eyes. "Good answer, Watson. I can see why you're so well respected around here."

Joanna's jade eyes flew wide in surprise. "I—what?"

"I said, *good answer*. You just passed your first test, Watson. I give a lot of pop quizzes in the OR, by the way. I like to keep my nurses on their toes."

Joanna breathed out a heavy sigh. She certainly hoped there wouldn't be any more "pop quizzes" tonight. The tension in the OR's sterile air was already thick enough as it was. And Dr. Wilkinson's—Harlan's—ice-blue stare was penetrating her.

Literally.

Joanna knew that behind the sterile surgical mask and face screen, the abrasive surgeon was undressing her with his eyes. Joanna could feel her crotch melting as she remembered their hot, anonymous tryst in the elevator, her body shuddering with the memory. She imagined the feeling of Harlan thrusting hard inside her. . .

Joanna bit her lip underneath her mask hard enough to draw blood. *Stop it,* she thought to herself. *This is an operating room, not a sex chamber. Stop having these unladylike thoughts this instant.*

"Watson? Are you all right?" Dr. Wilkinson's voice startled Joanna back to reality.

"Y-yes, Doctor," she stammered. "Shall I get you a new scalpel? The one you dropped is no longer sterile."

"Yes, do that, Joanna," Dr. Wilkinson said, using her given name for the first time since the operation began. The sound of her name escaping his lips was enough to set her cheeks aflame. She took several long, slow, deep breaths, mentally instructing her face, mind, and body to calm down, cool off, and get back to the task at hand.

Her face, mind, and body all refused.

It was going to be a very, very long operation.

Chapter Five

"GOD, I thought we were never going to get out of there," Joanna sighed to Shirley in the nurses' locker room once the operation was finally over.

Joanna glanced at her watch and noticed it was almost one a.m. She desperately needed to get some sleep, but there were still two hours left in her shift. She hoped there wouldn't be any more drunken frat boys coming in with broken legs this evening. After steeling herself against Harlan's piercing gaze in the OR for over four hours, it was all she could do just to keep her eyes open. She shucked off her dirty scrubs and stepped into the shower, turning the faucet all the way over to "COLD" in hopes it would wake her up. Not to mention calm her down.

"That man is evil," groaned Shirley, who had just stepped into the shower stall next to Joanna. A vaguely medicinal scent wafted over the ceramic stall divider as Shirley rinsed off the residue from the anesthesia machine. "Pure, unadulterated evil."

And in more ways than one, Shirley thought silently to herself, feeling tingling between her legs once more.

Joanna shivered under her own ice-cold shower stream—a futile attempt to keep her own raging libido at bay. "The guy's definitely obnoxious," she agreed. "But I wouldn't go so far as to call him *evil*."

Being a proper Southern lady, Joanna couldn't exactly call a man she'd just done the Wild Thing with evil. Coarse, ill-mannered, slimy, manipulative, and rude she could do. But not *evil*.

"Well, if I ever get spoken to like that in the OR again so help me God I will quit," Shirley hissed. "They don't pay me enough to put up with that kind of crap from anybody. I don't care how famous Dr. Wilkinson is—he needs to learn some manners."

Joanna shut off the tap with a jerk. She grabbed her towel and stepped out of her stall, then yanked open the curtain to Shirley's stall, nearly startling the poor naked woman out of her skin. "What's that? You say Dr. Wilkinson is *famous*?"

Shirley shut off her own faucet and wrapped herself in a towel. "Well, *duh*. What rock have you been hiding under, Joanna?"

Joanna scanned the files of her brain for her short list of world-famous surgeons. Dr. Harlan Wilkinson wasn't on it. Dr. Turnblatt had been well respected in and around the greater Raleigh-Durham metro region, but wasn't much known beyond that. Most of the other "famous" surgeons she'd heard of were nothing more than names of long-dead men in the pages of her dusty nursing texts, and most of them were from New York or New England, not her humble little hamlet of Statesville, North Carolina.

"Pardon me, Shirley, but I've never heard of Dr. Wilkinson before today. I guess I must have missed all his appearances on *David Letterman*, or whatever it is famous surgeons do to promote themselves these days."

Shirley sighed and shook her head as she tugged on a fresh set of scrubs. "Dr. Harlan Wilkinson is one of the most preeminent general surgeons in the entire country. Maybe even the world. He was on staff at Hofts University Medical Center in Boston before he came here. He's gotten recognition all over the world for his research. Plus, he spent time in Doctors Without Borders, serving in Somalia and Sierra Leone-"

Joanna put her hands on her still-damp hips. "How do you know all of this?"

Shirley rolled her eyes as she toweled herself off. "Joanna, it's only been the number-one topic of conversation around the hospital for the past month. Don't you pay attention at all? The hospital newsletter did a big spread on Dr. Wilkinson last month. You didn't see it?"

Between her double-overtime shifts under Doctor Turnblatt and the final stages of her divorce proceedings, Joanna hadn't paid much attention to the news. "I suppose not," she replied as she plucked a fresh set of scrubs from the hamper and tugged them on.

Shirley giggled. "Then I guess you didn't see the picture of him on the back of a Land Rover somewhere in the middle of Africa with his shirt off. *Yummy*."

Did that remark mean Shirley was homing in on Dr. Harlan Wilkinson's sex appeal too?

*How **dare** she*! Joanna thought. *That little **bitch**—*

Whoa. Wait a minute. Was it really possible that Joanna could she be that jealous and possessive of Harlan after *one* anonymous encounter in an elevator? By the way her eyes and back of her throat were burning, it certainly seemed that way. "I thought you said you didn't like him," she snapped, her voice almost a snarl.

"Oh, I don't," Shirley answered, slamming her locker shut. "Like I said, if you ask me, the man is pure, unadulterated evil. But that doesn't mean I don't think he's smoking hot. I mean, you'd practically have to be blind not to notice *that* about him."

Shirley certainly had a point there.

And Joanna was silently cursing herself for having had sex with the man in total darkness, thereby missing out on the treat of actually seeing Harlan Wilkinson's body in its delicious *au naturel* state.

"It's really a shame a gorgeous male physique like that is wasted on such a jerk," Shirley commented. "Don't you think so?"

Joanna didn't answer. Her cheeks smarting, she just smiled a big, fake grin and stomped out of the locker room.

Joanna plodded down the hallway towards the main nurses' station, grinding her teeth. What a mortifying nursing shift she'd just had! Not only was she getting screwed out of the precious time off the hospital had been promising her for months, she'd managed to screw her new boss's brains out, too. And now, the man whom she'd bestowed her precious sexual favors upon was screwing around with her mind—pretending like the whole thing never happened at all!

Joanna's stomach churned at the notion of having to set eyes on Dr. Harlan Wilkinson again. At one level, the man made her sick. And at another, the man made her want to take her panties off in public.

It was enough to make a girl get all hot and bothered.

As much as Joanna wanted to dash out of the hospital (so she could crawl under the nearest rock and die), that was impossible. With two hours left on her shift, Joanna had to get back to work, like it or not—or else Mr. Personality just might make good on his promise to write her up for disciplinary action.

Joanna shuddered to think at just what that write-up would look like in her Personnel file.

It would probably go something like this: "I, Harlan Wilkinson, MD, wish to formally reprimand Joanna Watson, RN, for getting snippy with me in the OR because I pretended we hadn't just made love five minutes before conducting our first surgical operation together."

That wouldn't exactly help her come annual raise time, would it?

Joanna made a mental note to start working on her resume.

*****

The rest of Joanna's shift passed without incident. She remained on call at her station just outside the main operating room, in a fresh set of sterile scrubs just in case she should be called back in for any emergency surgeries. She kept her eyes glued to a television mounted on the recovery room wall, staring at the late-night infomercial it blared at full volume in hopes that it would serve as enough stimulus to keep her awake for just a few hours more. By 1:45 a.m., her eyes were bloodshot, her eyelids heavy, and her head was throbbing with a migraine.

Her crotch was throbbing, too. Her body was making it clear to her that it wanted another dose of the very special medicine that

Dr. Harlan Wilkinson had served up to her in the elevator hours before.

Damn it. That was the last thing she needed right now.

At 1:57, Joanna figured she was safe to pack up and go home. She was exhausted. And even if she got home quickly, she'd only have about five hours to sleep before having to report back to the hospital for her next regular shift.

Joanna flipped the television off and started walking back towards the nurses' locker room to gather her things. But she hadn't made it three steps before she heard a gruff voice echo on the linoleum just behind her.

"You still have two minutes left on your shift, Watson."

Joanna spun around. Harlan's azure eyes were bright as lasers even in the dimmed hallway lights, and they bore into her like knives. "Oh, come on, Doctor. I've been on duty for sixteen straight hours. Two minutes aren't that big a deal at this point—"

Harlan's eyes narrowed. "Yes, they are. In medicine, every minute—every *second*—counts. Those two extra minutes you spend high-tailing it out of here could be the difference between life and death for a patient who arrives in the surgery department with a hemorrhaging artery."

"With all due respect, Doctor, I don't see any hemorrhaging patients hereabouts," Joanna replied coolly. "Do you?"

"That's beside the point," he said, taking a step closer to her. Even from more than ten feet away, she could swear she felt the heat rising from his body against the bare skin of her forearms, making her break out into girlish goose pimples. She absently rubbed at her arms – which only turned them into giant erogenous zones.

"Watson, what I'm trying to emphasize here is that I expect one hundred percent from my nurses one hundred percent of the time," he barked. "No slacking off on my watch. Not even for two minutes."

Joanna glanced at the gray steel clock mounted on the hallway wall. She watched as the second hand finished its rotation, then glanced back at Harlan, her eyes locking with his. "Well, the last two minutes of my shift are up. I don't see any dying patients in the vicinity, and I also see my shift replacement coming around the corner. So if it will suit you and your out-of-control ego, Dr. Harlan Wilkinson, I will be going now. I have an urgent appointment with my bed."

With that tender expression of Carolina hospitality, Joanna turned on her heel and headed back to the locker room without giving Harlan a second glance.

Four minutes later, Joanna was in the hospital parking garage. As she fumbled the key into the lock of her battered old Honda, she heard the heavy metal door of the stairwell slam shut, followed by the click of hard-soled shoes on asphalt. Momentarily terrified that a serial rapist had somehow followed her out to her car, Joanna froze, unable even to unlock the door to get into the relative safety of her vehicle.

"Relax," came a familiar male voice from across the parking structure. "It's just me, Watson. Believe it or not, my out-of-control ego and I have to sleep, too."

Joanna's felt her cheeks color. Was there no escaping this man? She managed to get her car door open and tossed her purse and duffel bag into the passenger seat. She tried to coax her body into the car after them, but her feet had somehow glued themselves to the concrete floor of the parking garage.

And all at once, her entire lower half went into flames.

Joanna's body was ripe and raring to go for another impromptu lovemaking session, whether she liked it or not.

Harlan seemed to pick up on this right away. "So what's the holdup, Watson?" He chuckled. "If you're as tired as you say you are, why don't you just go home?"

"I—" was Joanna's stammering reply. Her mouth went cottony when she caught sight of the bulge in Harlan's pants. Even in the dim, smoky light of the darkened parking garage, Joanna could make out a tent in the man's pants worthy of a three-ring circus.

Harlan inched closer. "You know, I'd really like to join you on that urgent appointment you have with your bed," he said. "I think a nice long stay in your bed would do the both of us a world of good. Unless you'd prefer to get busy right here."

Joanna stiffened. She tried once more to get in her car and drive away, and couldn't. The more she stared at Harlan, the more she wanted to stay right where she was.

The whole situation was way out of hand.

Joanna slapped herself across the face. She had to nip this thing in the bud. She just *had* to. Joanna was a proper Southern lady. She had manners and decorum. She'd gone to her marriage bed a virgin, after all. What the hell was she doing in a parking garage in the middle of the night, seconds away from letting an arrogant, rude, uncivilized Yankee—not to mention her new boss—screw her brains out up against the side of a car?

And why the hell was she so damn excited at the prospect?

She was losing her mind.

Now Harlan's body was pressed up against hers. She could feel his arousal, hard and throbbing and insistent against her left thigh. She could smell it, too—that unmistakable coppery, musky, manly scent of sex enveloped her like a fog. "So what's it gonna be, Watson?" Harlan whispered. "Are we gonna do this thing, or are we just gonna call it a night and go home?"

"I—I don't know," she stammered. And it was true. She was at a total loss. Did she listen to her heaving body and take the sexual satisfaction that was being served up to her on a platter, or did she do the rational, reasonable thing and get the hell away from there?

It was pretty hard to listen to reason when she was on fire.

Joanna's whole body vibrated from intense need. The instincts driving Joanna's actions that night were purely primal—raw, animalistic, primitive. They made no sense, but they didn't have to.

Joanna's right hand floated down to the waist of her scrubs as if propelled by invisible machinery. She tried again to stop herself, but couldn't. Her body had taken on a will of its own.

With two quick flicks of her wrist and fingers, her scrub bottoms puddled around her ankles. She made a move to pull her panties to the side, but Harlan had already beat her to it. He reached into one of his pockets and pulled out a condom, which he whisked on in a blink of an eye. Before she could even realize what was happening,

Joanna was flipped over facedown onto the hood of her Honda with Harlan inside her.

Joanna had never done anything like this before. Casual sex across the hood of a car in a parking garage? It just didn't seem real. She'd always been a strait-laced, demure, missionary-position-in-bed-under-the-covers kind of girl. And it wasn't as if her impotent ex-husband had been capable of introducing her to much else.

Harlan was so huge and was thrusting so deep, Joanna honestly thought he might thrust himself all the way through her body.

And Joanna didn't think that would be a bad thing, either.

Harlan's strokes were hard and fast, each one vibrating her entire being. All at once, Joanna came hard, completely without warning. Joanna bit into the flesh of her left arm to keep from screaming. She couldn't risk anyone inside the hospital building hearing her cry out in ecstasy. She'd lose her job. She'd be humiliated, the laughing-stock scarlet woman of the whole town. But even so, the knowledge that she was making love with a man in public—that she could get caught at any time—was more thrilling than anything she'd ever experienced.

Anything but the wild ride Harlan was giving her right now, anyway.

Joanna had been desperate for some real, red-hot sex for her entire life. And now, she was finally having some. The fact that she was having some with her arrogant S.O.B. of a new boss in a public parking garage was merely a minor inconvenience.

Joanna lifted her chest up off the hood of her Honda and braced herself on her forearms. She wanted the last few moments to be the deepest, hardest, most intense of all—and she could tell from the sound of Harlan's breathing that his orgasm was close. She raised her rump up off the hood and into the air at the steepest angle she could muster just as Harlan thrust into her for the final time. This time, Harlan hit Joanna's G-spot at the exact moment he exploded—sending her over the edge one final time in an interstellar leap of her own.

Harlan collapsed on top of Joanna, pressing her into the dirty, dingy hood of her rattling old Honda. Hardly a romantic afterglow, but that didn't matter. This coupling was never about romance in the first place.

Harland withdrew and rearranged his pants. "Thanks, Watson," he said, all business again. "I'll see you back here tomorrow."

Joanna was stunned. "But—"

Harlan tipped an imaginary hat at her, a poor Yankee attempt at being a Southern gentleman. "What happens here, stays here," he said. "Good night." Then he turned on his heel and headed for his car. He was gone before she could get dressed.

Joanna got dressed and sighed. She was mortified—again. Was this really what casual sex was supposed to be like? She had no experience in such matters. She didn't know what to think, how to react. No proper Southern lady let a stranger screw her over the hood of a car—let alone enjoyed it as much as she just had.

At one level, she was hurt that Harlan had done a classic "wham-bam, thank you ma'am" and hightailed it out of there as fast as he could. But at another level, it seemed like a perfectly natural way for him to end things. Did she really expect Harlan to cuddle her and stay the night on the hood of her car? That would have been ridiculous.

The question remained—how was a formerly proper, demure Southern lady supposed to act now that she'd slept with her boss twice in one workday, and *liked* it? How did former Southern belles blend back into polite society once they'd had wild sex on the hoods of their late-model cars?

They didn't have a chapter on that back at charm school, that was for sure.

Chapter Six

SHIRLEY DANIELS had never understood what made Joanna Watson tick. And she didn't expect to start now.

Shirley was still in the locker room, too stunned at Joanna's sudden exit to finish getting dressed. What had she said to make the woman so mad? All Shirley did was comment on Dr. Harlan Wilkinson's hot bod—which the man had in spades, asshole or not—and Joanna Watson had acted as if Shirley had punched her in the face.

What the hell was up that woman's butt, anyway?

What, indeed. Shirley figured it probably had to do with Dr. Harlan Wilkinson. The man certainly seemed to have an effect on people. On women, especially.

And Shirley figured if the man could turn her—a cold, frigid fish if there ever was one—into a buzzing bundle of nerves, she could hardly imagine the effect the Yankee surgeon was having on the beautiful, sensual—and freshly divorced—Joanna Watson.

Hell, for all she knew, the two of them were probably off having sex over the hood of a car somewhere.

But Shirley wasn't going to let that bother her. She wasn't the jealous type. And she had business of her own to take care of.

Shirley headed out of the locker room to check the OR duty roster. She silently thanked God when she saw there were no more operations scheduled for the day. And she wasn't needed at her parents' nursing home tonight, either—for once. Finally, after weeks of double shifts and long nights caring for her decrepit parents, she could go home at a decent hour and give her tired feet and back a rest.

But going home for a rest was the last thing on her mind.

For once in a very long while, Shirley Daniels had a free evening to spend however she liked. She'd been looking forward to this free time all week—even if she'd had absolutely no idea what to do with it.

Until now.

The melty buzz that was fast growing in Shirley as she skipped up and down Covington Community Hospital's twisting, dingy hallways towards the parking garage told her exactly what she would be doing with her free evening. When she finally made it to her car and slid her key into the ignition, she knew there was no arguing with the burning desire inside her.

Tonight, Shirley Daniels would have sex.

The only problem was, she had no idea how to go about making that happen.

It had been so long since Shirley had gone out on a date—or even cruised for good-looking guys at a local bar—that she was totally clueless about how to attract a man, let alone find one willing to sleep with her. And it wasn't as if Statesville, North Carolina had a swinging singles scene. There were only two options for meeting single men in this godforsaken town: at the Dew Drop Bar on Main Street (which wasn't much of an option, unless she was desperate enough to go home with toothless old men with faded Navy tattoos and tobacco juice in their beards); or at the First Pentecostal Church of the Nazarene's weekly Singles Supper (not an option either, since Shirley was an atheist).

It looked like Shirley would have to get the hell out of Statesville if she wanted to get laid tonight. Either that, or she'd have to hire a professional.

She checked her watch. Eleven thirty. The night was still young. And she wasn't due back at the hospital until eleven a.m. the next morning. Plenty of time for her to make an overnight trip to partake in a little big-city action in Raleigh. Or maybe some tight college-boy action in Chapel Hill. Both options sounded equally tempting.

She was freshly showered and wearing her tightest pair of Levi's and a new halter top. She always kept a makeup kit in her glove box, so she could be glammed up in no time. She had a brand-new pack of Trojans in her purse, so she was ready for action. And if she wore her hair down, she could easily pass for someone ten years younger. Plenty young enough to attract some hot college-boy attention.

Shirley started the car and checked her roadway map for the quickest route to Chapel Hill. As an alumna of the university there, she knew where to find the frat houses and college bars that were sure to be chock-full of horny, red-blooded American boys who would be all too eager to bed an older woman, even on a school night.

Shirley's body was a live wire for the entire ninety-minute drive to Chapel Hill. By the time she rolled into the center of the college town, it was almost one in the morning, and the houses on Fraternity Row were mostly dark. But there was still one fraternity house lit up with the bright lights of a weeknight college party left on the block—the Sigma Nu house, all the way at the end of the campus' main drag.

A slow smile spread across Shirley's face. She remembered the Sigma Nu house. She remembered it well.

Because believe it or not, there was a very brief time in Shirley Daniels's life when she was not the cold frigid fish with no social life that she was today. Fifteen-odd years ago, when she was a coed on the University of North Carolina's campus, she was a bright young freshman pledge at the UNC Chi Omega chapter looking for a frat boy to accompany her to her sorority's Enchanted Spring social. She'd found her date (and so much more) within the walls of the Sigma Nu house—and that date had been the boy she'd given her precious virginity to. They dated for three years, breaking up just before Shirley graduated from nursing school. But they'd parted on good terms, and Shirley had always thought fondly of the handsome young fellow who'd been the vehicle for her sexual awakening.

And now, at age thirty-four, Shirley Daniels was undergoing a second sexual awakening of sorts. Why not go full-circle and pick up her boy-toy in the very same frat house where she'd been deflowered up against a wall more than fifteen years ago? For old times' sake.

She had plenty of years of fruitless, frustrating celibacy to make up for, after all.

Shirley parked the car, checked her makeup in the rearview mirror, and took a deep breath for courage.

She needed plenty of courage for what she was about to do.

Shirley marched up to the frat house's front door and banged the heavy brass knocker. She had to bang it several times to be heard over the thumping bass and loud voices of the party within, but she finally got an answer.

The most beautiful twenty-year-old she'd ever seen opened the front door. He had a pair of stunning ice-blue eyes, which looked her up and down, then twinkled. Obviously he liked what he saw.

"Hey, what's up?" the boy-toy asked in a deep, gravelly voice that sounded much older than its owner's tender years. "Wanna party?"

"You know I do," Shirley chirped.

She swept past him into the swooping front foyer she remembered so well from all the visits she'd made to the Sigma Nu house in college. A quick glance around showed her that even after fifteen years, almost nothing in this testosterone-soaked house of hedonism had changed. She recognized the beat-up, duct-taped brown leather couch as the very same one where she'd shared late-night drunken trysts with her very own Sigma Nu pledge so many years ago, along with the grimy, scuffed walls and the piles of empty beer bottles and pizza boxes that were the signature décor of frat boys the world over. In a way, she almost felt as if she'd come home from a long, hard journey.

And in a way, she had.

The blue-eyed boy-toy who'd let her in handed her an ice-cold beer. "So what's your name?" he asked. "I haven't seen you around here before."

"I'm Shirley," she replied, extended her hand, which the blue-eyed boy-toy bent over and kissed like a true Southern gentleman. "And I'm a graduate of this fine university. I was just passing through Chapel Hill and thought I'd drop in and see some friends of mine here at Sigma Nu. I'm ahhh—an old friend of the chapter."

Never mind how old, Shirley thought to herself.

The boy-toy's blue eyes sparkled. "Really? I'll have to ask some of my senior frat brothers if they know you, then. I'm Jason. I'm a sophomore. I just pledged this spring, so I'm still getting to know everybody around here."

Ah, a *sophomore*. Young and fresh, but not a mere child, either. And a new pledge that she could ply with stories of her long-ago escapades in this very frat house.

This one's ripe for the picking, Shirley thought as she mentally planned out what exactly she'd like to do with Jason's lithe young body.

Still, she had to be careful. It had been so long since Shirley had been with a man, it paid to be very cautious.

The party was breaking up. The drunken frat boys that hadn't already passed out on couches or the floor started pairing up with sorority girls and disappearing into their rooms. Jason cast a sidelong glance at Shirley, then teetered nervously back and forth on the balls of his feet. "Well, um, it's getting kind of late," he said. "The party's starting to wind down already. Normally we'd party a lot later, but the chapter got into trouble with the dean last semester for making too much noise on weeknights, so we're trying to chill out and quiet down a little. Sorry you're missing all the fun."

Shirley downed her beer in one gulp. "Oh Jason, honey," she cooed. "The fun's just getting started."

With that, she grabbed Jason by the collar and led him up Sigma Nu's huge, creaking wooden staircase. When they reached the first landing she turned to face him. "Now if memory serves me correctly, the sophomore pledges stay on the third floor in the group dorm. Is that still true?"

Jason nodded, gape-mouthed. "How do you know so much about my frat?"

Shirley smiled and batted her eyelashes. "Let's just say I'm an old, old friend of Sigma Nu and leave it at that."

Jason polished his own beer off and shrugged. He'd obviously figured out that he was about to get laid, and that was all that mattered to him.

And getting laid was all that mattered to Shirley, too. "Do you have any roommates up there?" she asked. "Because if you do, they're going to get an eyeful." She dragged him up the second flight of stairs and into the large dorm room filled with bunk beds she remembered so well from her own sophomore year so long ago. Shirley and her old Sigma Nu boyfriend Ted had done the nasty seven ways to Sunday on those rickety old metal bunks back in the early '90s, and now she had a chance to make those very same bunks sing a new song with a boy-toy almost half her age.

It was enough to make a girl all hot and bothered.

They made it to the third floor. The dorm was empty. "I've only got three roommates this semester, and all three of them are downstairs passed out drunk," Jason said. "Looks like we'll have this place to ourselves 'til morning."

"Excellent." Without another word, Shirley clamped her mouth over Jason's and sucked his bottom lip hard enough to draw it all the way into her mouth. Then she gave each and every one of his teeth a full dental exam with the tip of her tongue, followed by an archeological dig of his throat. By the time they both finally came up for air, the twenty-year-old frat boy was shaking at the knees.

"W-Wow," he whispered, breathless. "You are one awesome kisser. What'd you say your name was again?"

"Never mind," Shirley replied, and shoved him backwards onto a cot. "Just take your pants off."

"O—okay," Jason stammered, and fumbled with his fly. Now he was out-and-out trembling, so much so that he couldn't even work his own zipper.

Well, Shirley would just have to take care of that herself.

Surprised at her own dexterity, Shirley had Jason's pants and boxers off with just a few flicks of her wrist, and was awestruck at the sight of Jason's manhood pointing straight up at the heavens.

It had been years since Shirley had done anything sexual. *Years.* And yet, here in this familiar place, Shirley felt transported back to the glorious, carefree days of her youth. She felt almost as if her body had been hijacked by strange, unseen forces that were guiding her every move, helping to make up for the fact that she'd gotten so rusty in the sex department after so many years of doing nothing but work double shifts and care for her aging parents. Giving this trembling, naïve fratboy the best night of his short life was liberating for Shirley in more ways than one.

"Who the hell are you, anyway?" Jason sputtered after he collected himself. "And where have you been all my life?"

"Never you mind who I am," she breathed. "Just do what I ask, and I guarantee tonight will be the best night of your life.

When her boy-toy was finally spent, Shirley tried to entertain him with some war stories of her own escapades in and around the Sigma Nu house during the early-'90s grunge era. But before she could get three words out, Jason was stone dead asleep.

Shirley felt more energized than she'd been in years. Sleep was the absolute last thing on her mind.

Feeling a bit naughty for "loving and leaving," Shirley dressed and prepared to leave. Just before she did, she penned a good-bye note to Jason on a scrap of paper she found underneath his cot. It read:

Dear Jason,
Thanks for a wonderful time. We'll have to do this again sometime.
With love,
A SEXY OL' CHI-O

Chi-O. It had been more than a decade since Shirley had referred to herself by her old sorority's nickname, but it seemed appropriate. After all, back in her day, the ladies of UNC's Chi Omega chapter were known as the best lovers on campus.

Shirley wondered if she might soon become known as the best lover at Covington Community Hospital, too.

She could always try.

Chapter Seven

JOANNA'S ALARM clock jolted her awake at seven thirty a.m. She had already overslept. How many times had she hit the snooze bar? Five? Six? She had a little less than half and hour to shower, dress, and arrive at work for her next shift. As she headed for the bathroom, she said a silent prayer that her fellow surgical nurse Lindsay Strouse had recovered from the flu so Joanna wouldn't have to get dragged into any more extra surgery shifts herself. An easy, quiet, stress-free stint behind the nurses' station—the "break" Administration had long promised her—was all Joanna had the energy for today. Plus, it was unlikely that Harlan would cross her path there. If he was like most surgeons, he'd give the mind-numbing paperwork and dripping bedpans of the ordinary duty nurses a wide berth.

And a wide berth from Harlan was exactly what she needed. She could hardly afford to cross paths with him today. Because it seemed every time she did, she ended up dropping her drawers. Not exactly a good career move.

Joanna stepped into the shower and turned the taps all the way over to "HOT". She stood stock-still underneath the scalding water, not soaping or shampooing herself, just enjoying the heat and steam for a few fleeting moments. Even as she looked forward to her easy nurses' station shift, Joanna had the feeling that this one minute of relaxation was the only down time she'd enjoy all day.

As if on cue, Joanna heard her phone ring. Agitated, she jumped out of the shower without bothering to wrap a towel around herself, and dripped water all over the carpet as she made a dash for the hallway phone.

"Hello?"

"Watson, why the hell aren't you at the hospital?" growled a familiar male voice.

"Harlan—I mean, Dr. Wilkinson? Is that you?"

"Of course it's me," was his terse reply. "I'm calling to find out where the hell you are."

"I'm standing in my front hall." Joanna's voice was clipped. What business was it of his where she was right now? Her shift didn't start until eight o' clock, and she wasn't slated to be on surgery duty, anyway. And she wasn't about to become anybody's booty call.

"Well, get the hell out of your front hall and get the hell over here," Harlan seethed, and hung up the phone before Joanna had a chance to reply.

Joanna slammed down the receiver so hard she almost knocked her telephone table over. The nerve of that egotistical bastard! The *nerve*. She wasn't due in to work yet. And she wasn't exactly in the mood for an early-morning wham-bam-thank-you-ma'am with him, either. Especially given the fact he was acting like a troll.

Well, she'd show him. She'd take her sweet time getting over to Covington Community Hospital that morning. She'd laze into the duty nurses' station at 8:01, and wouldn't even bother to show her face in Surgery and Recovery unless Maryam Malone or a senior member of hospital administration ordered her to. She didn't care what that S.O.B. Dr. Harlan Wilkinson said his contract gave him the right to do—he wasn't going to get away with ordering her around. No siree.

"I'll show that rat bastard a thing or two," Joanna said aloud as she went to her bedroom to get dressed.

There. That made her feel better. That calmed her down enough to keep from putting her fist through her bedroom wall.

Or did it?

As Joanna pulled on her bra and panties, she felt again the familiar warmth that had crept into her groin the day before, along with a heavy tension in her chest and a hot, rapid throbbing between her ears. It felt vaguely like a panic attack, but Joanna had never been one to get panicked just before going to work.

No, it felt much more like a case of The Hornies.

Like it or not, Joanna's body was screaming for another quickie. *Damn it*. This just could not be happening again.

Joanna stumbled back into the bathroom to splash some cold water onto her face. Even after a good soaking in the icy water, her face still felt hot. She stared at her reflection in the mirror and saw that her cheeks were still flushed—red as ripe crabapples, in fact—and her eyelids half-closed in an expression that was pure sexuality.

Oh no, Joanna thought as she stared at herself in the mirror. At that moment, she knew why she felt so out of sorts. She knew why the pit of her stomach melted and quavered at the mere thought of Dr. Harlan Wilkinson, no matter how rude he might be with her. No matter how much of an ill-mannered, conceited oaf he was, no matter how much he played cavalier with hospital regulations, no matter what kind of hard time he gave her in the OR, at that moment Joanna Watson knew she was falling for him.

She was falling, and falling hard, whether she liked it or not.

And that, of course, set up a whole separate set of issues when it came to Dr. Harlan Wilkinson's potential as a romantic partner.

Ever since she and her husband Bob had separated three years ago, she'd thought off and on about trying to find love—or even lust—again, but no one had sparked so much as a second glance on her part until Harlan crossed her path.

And he had done a lot more than spark a second glance. He had awakened sensations in Joanna's body that she'd never known existed. But with the now-constant dampness between her legs, with the way her heartbeat sped up whenever she imagined his rugged, razor-stubbled face—she knew that at the very least, *lust* had found her. A lust that absolutely must be satisfied.

But as Joanna dragged herself over to her closet to pick out a fresh set of nurses' attire, she knew that even satisfying her growing lust for the globetrotting surgeon would not be enough. Having him in her bed wouldn't do enough to cool the heated pounding between her ears or the pulsing ache in her nether parts. No, just having Dr. Harlan Wilkinson in her bed wouldn't be enough, not at all.

Somehow, Joanna knew, she would have to win Dr. Harlan Wilkinson's heart, too.

Not an easy task, to be sure, because from what she'd seen of him so far, Harlan didn't *have* a heart.

Chapter Eight

"You're late." Maryam Malone's sweet-yet-authoritative voice greeted Joanna at the nursing station just as she arrived.

Joanna glanced at her watch. 8:02. *Good*, she thought. Two whole minutes past the start of her shift. That ought to fix Harlan's over-blown ego-wagon nicely. "I'm only two minutes late," Joanna replied. "I'm sorry, but I got delayed by a few minutes when that rat bastard Dr. Wilkinson called me at home and pulled me out of the shower."

Joanna was careful not to mention that the mere thought of Harlan turned her knees to jelly. And she didn't think Maryam needed to know how many times she and her new boss had already done the Horizontal Bop, either.

Maryam chuckled. "I see you have had the pleasure of making Darth Vader's acquaintance. Has he tried the old Jedi Mind Trick on you yet?"

Joanna pulled off her light jacket and tossed it over the back of the nurses' station chair. *You have no idea*, she thought silently to herself. "I didn't know you knew so much about *Star Wars*, Maryam."

"I learned everything I ever needed to know about *Star Wars* from my grandsons," the seasoned old nurse explained. "Enough to know that Dr. Wilkinson answers to the Dark Side, at any rate. He's been looking for you all morning, by the way. And judging by his mood, he's not happy that you didn't come in at the crack of dawn like he did. I suppose that's why he called you at home."

Joanna smirked. "I suppose so. How did he get my number, I wonder?"

Maryam shifted anxiously on her sneakered feet. "I gave him your number. I hope you don't mind."

Joanna stared at her, incredulous. "Why did you do that?"

Maryam smiled. "Sorry, but I couldn't help it. He used the Jedi Mind Trick on me."

"I see." Joanna gritted her teeth. Now thanks to Maryam's unwitting participation, she figured she'd now be Harlan's personal twenty-four-hour booty call for the forseeable future. Not that it would be a bad thing, but. . .

Joanna blinked her eyes several times, trying to clear her mind of the image of Harlan's body. She was at work, and her job as a nurse was serious business. She simply could not allow out-of-control blind lust to cloud her judgment on the job any longer.

Joanna composed herself, pulled the morning's patient files out of the plastic wall tray and started shuffling through them. "Maryam, I hope you told him after the Jedi Mind Trick wore off that I'm already assigned to regular nurses' station duty for the next two weeks, and am therefore off-limits in the operating room. Unless Lindsay Strouse never comes back from sick leave, that is. By the way, is she getting better?"

"She's back today, actually."

"Good," Joanna replied. "Then she can go deal with Dr. Wilkinson herself. I'm not in the mood." A lie. But she couldn't exactly tell Maryam the truth. The truth would just get her fired.

Nurse Malone pulled up an extra chair and sat down. "Well, there's kind of a thing you and I will have to talk about on that score," she said, a nervous edge to her voice. "You see, it doesn't really matter one way or the other that Lindsay's back from sick leave. You're on surgery duty anyway. *Double-shift* surgery duty. Maybe even triple, if need be."

Joanna's breath caught. "What?"

"I'm sorry to be the bearer of bad news, Joanna, I really am." Maryam sighed and shook her head. "But Dr. Wilkinson's gone over my head to Administration and ordered the powers that be to put you at his disposal at all times. You're off nurses' station duty until further notice. From now on, you're on call twenty-four/seven, and you report only to Dr. Harlan Wilkinson. You might even say that he *owns* you."

Owned her? Harlan *owned* her?

Joanna bit her lip. Although she'd already figured after last night that it was only a matter of time before something like this happened, she hadn't expected it so soon. Clearly, this threw a wrench into Joanna's plan to beat both him and his heart of stone into womanly submission.

Maryam gave Joanna's shoulder a maternal squeeze. "You should probably head over to Surgery now," she said. "I can manage the nurse's station until Lindsay can get herself over here. Good luck, Joanna. Trust me, you're going to need it."

"Thanks," was Joanna's reply as she left to face her surely-coming doom.

*****

Joanna arrived in the Surgery and Recovery wing about five minutes later, dragging her jacket and duffel bag behind her. She dreaded facing Dr. Harlan Wilkinson more and more at every step. Her entire body quaked with fear and desire. How could she ever have thought herself capable of taming him? How could she have imagined herself able to suppress the lust that had overtaken her body and annihilated all of her ladylike Southern good sense? How was she going to suppress the irresistible urge to drop her drawers and open her legs as soon as she laid eyes on him?

God only knew.

Joanna took a deep breath, and decided that the best course of action was like removing a Band-Aid—a nasty job best gotten over with quickly. She trudged up to the Chief of Surgery's closed office door and knocked on the opaque glass.

After a moment, it opened. Dr. Harlan Wilkinson regarded her with a mixture of relief and contempt. Unlike the rumpled scrubs, disheveled hair, and nine o'clock shadow he bore yesterday during their first encounter, today he was clean-shaven, neatly coiffed, and outfitted in a crisp white oxford, pressed blue slacks, and an immaculately knotted red silk tie. A stethoscope was draped around his neck, and he wore a loose-fitting white lab coat over his obviously expensive, custom-tailored clothes. He looked more like a laid-back family doctor than a chief hospital surgeon.

"I see you've finally made it in, Watson," he said, his voice about as warm and welcoming as your average meat freezer.

Joanna shot him a look as frigid as his tone. "I was scheduled to arrive at eight a.m. today, and I arrived at eight a.m. I don't know where you get the idea that I'm late, Doctor."

"You arrived at eight-oh-two," Dr. Wilkinson snapped back. "I had Nurse Malone call me and tell me the exact time you showed up, and that's the answer she gave me. So yes, you were indeed late. Although I'm sure Maryam Malone has already acquainted you with your new work arrangements, and from now on I expect you to be on call twenty-four/seven. I've requisitioned a beeper for you from Supply, you should have that shortly. Until you get the beeper, however, I suggest you set yourself up with a cot over in the residents' sleeping quarters. That way, I'll know I can rely on you to be here anytime I need you, day or night."

Joanna blinked twice. Did this maddening man really expect her to be at his beck and call *twenty-four hours a day*? To the point she was expected to *move into* the hospital—sleeping, eating, and bathing here just like some kind of prisoner? Not to mention becoming his own personal twenty-four-hour, on-site booty call?

Ha. Not if she could help it.

"Dr. Wilkinson, with all due respect, there is no amount of money this hospital could pay me to get me to move in to residents' sleeping quarters and work twenty-four hours a day. I'm sorry, but that's just outrageous."

Harlan's eyes narrowed. He folded his arms across his chest. "You were willing to put that kind of time in for my predecessor. So why not me?"

Joanna was taken aback at this. On-site booty call, indeed. The incorrigible man would be lucky if he ever caught sight of Joanna's bare-naked body again.

"I pulled all those extra shifts for Dr. Turnblatt as a personal favor to him," Joanna answered, locking her verdant eyes with Dr. Wilkinson's azure ones to show her defiance. "I didn't have to, and he didn't make me. I worked for Dr. Turnblatt for many years, and I respected him enough to know that he was paying me a compliment when he requested I support him on all those surgeries. And I will also have you know that he made all the shift arrangements with me in advance, and never once required me to wear a beeper or make the hospital my primary residence. I happen to have a nice condo to live in, Dr. Wilkinson, not to mention a personal life." (She said this despite the fact that since her divorce, her so-called "personal life" consisted mostly of spending her nights alone in front of the television eating microwaved Lean Cuisines.)

Dr. Wilkinson's expression softened. "Why do you think my request you work all this extra time is any less of a compliment coming from me than it was from Dr. Turnblatt?" Dr. Wilkinson's ice-blue eyes took on a slightly suggestive glaze, and Joanna could swear she caught those eyes dip to catch a glance of her bosom. Was Harlan really insinuating that she had given the elderly, dried-up old Dr. Turnblatt the same sexual favors she'd bestowed on him?

The bastard. She wanted to slap him. "Just what are you implying, Dr. Wilkinson?"

A slow smile spread across Dr. Wilkinson's chiseled features. "I'm not implying anything untoward, Watson, believe me. I was trying to make a joke. There's this great new thing called laughing. You should really try it."

Joanna smoothed the front of her nurse's uniform with her hands and turned her attentions to the pile of incoming surgery patient files. "Sorry, Doctor, but I'm not amused."

"Joanna, what I'm trying to say is, I am requesting all these extra hours and service from you because I know you can handle it."

Joanna. He'd said her given name. The mere act of those three syllables escaping Harlan's lips was enough to set her pulse to racing. Damn, what was this man doing to her? Joanna pretended to be interested in the file of a sixty-eight-year-old triple-bypass patient due in for surgery the next day, but the heat brewed in her chest at every word he uttered.

"You did some damn fine nursing in the OR yesterday," Harlan went on. Joanna couldn't tell if he noticed her aroused state or not, but if he did, he didn't comment on it. "*Damn* fine. Some of the best I've ever seen, in fact. What's more, you stood up to me without batting an eyelash. Do you know how many nurses there are in this world willing to do that? None. I don't know if you've noticed, but I'm not the friendliest person."

"No, I hadn't noticed that at all, Doctor." Joanna's voice was nothing but a croak. She could feel that Harlan had taken a step closer to her. He was behind her, just inches away. She could feel the heat of his torso. She could feel the feathery touch of his breath against the nape of her neck. She felt an invisible connection growing between them, a line of sensual electricity that was just barely there, but present enough to make her insides quiver, to make her nether parts wet, to make her head so heavy with desire she could hardly remain standing. It was all she could do to keep breathing. And still, Harlan's warm breath was there, lapping at the back of her neck like a babbling brook.

"I think you're lying." He was so close behind her now, his breath on her neck felt almost like a kiss.

Joanna stepped away from him abruptly, almost ready to lose control. But she wouldn't, *couldn't* show him a moment's weakness.

Joanna backed up against the front panel of the refrigerator just outside the office used to store blood plasma. "Dr. Wilkinson, with all due respect, I hardly think it is appropriate or professional for you to accuse me of lying when I was merely stating a fact about our working relationship, which I frankly do not find in any way out of the ordinary."

A boldfaced lie, of course. Joanna's voice was quavering so much now she could hardly get the words out at all.

Harlan gave her an odd look. "Watson, are you sure you're all right?"

Joanna forced a smile. "Of course I'm all right. I'm fine. What makes you think I'm not?" Now Joanna's voice sounded low, hoarse and breathy. She was mortified at the sound of it.

"Watson, you sound aroused."

So much for getting the upper hand.

Joanna cleared her throat, willing herself to speak in a normal tone of voice. "Dr. Wilkinson, that is a *completely* inappropriate thing to say to your lead surgical nurse. If you *ever* make a comment like that to me again, I swear I'll—"

"Write me up for sexual harrassment? That might be kind of hard, given what you and I did yesterday. Twice." Although his voice was hard and serious, Harlan shot her a boyish grin that showed her he was joking. Joanna couldn't help but chuckle.

"Ah, I see you've finally heard about that great new laughing thing," he chuckled. "How's it working out for you?"

Joanna stopped laughing and set her jaw. "Dr. Wilkinson, would you mind returning to the task at hand? I was hoping you could brief me on the patients you'll be operating on today so I can assist you in the OR to the best of my nursing abilities."

Harlan's features hardened a little and his body stiffened. He seemed disappointed, perhaps even a little angry that Joanna was purposefully backing away from him. Maybe she was finally going about this delicate dance of seduction in the right way. (Which was kind of backwards, considering that she'd already slept with the man twice. But better late than never.)

Joanna silently scolded herself for marrying the first man who'd ever shown an interest in her—Bob, her impotent, possessive, and (thankfully) now ex-husband—instead of "playing the field" more. Joanna was in way over her head.

"Watson, I was really hoping to get to know you a little better before we got started this morning," Dr. Wilkinson said after what seemed like an eternity. "I like to get to know my nurses as people."

"Well, you already know me in the Biblical sense," Joanna snapped. "Isn't that enough?"

He ignored this. "I find it helps improve my working relationship with my lead nurse if I know what makes her tick. But it seems to me that you'd prefer to keep everything strictly business. And that's fine. I suppose." He went to gather some files from his desk.

You suppose? Joanna thought, indignant. *Are you going to give up that easily, Dr. Harlan Wilkinson? Aren't you even going to make an effort to get to know me better? Am I really that uninteresting?*

Yes, she *was* that uninteresting. Obviously, the only things the man thought she was good for were holding scalpels and having sex with strangers over the hood of a car.

As Joanna listened to Harlan shuffle through the day's scheduled surgical cases with the stone-cold, efficient manner of the average executioner, Joanna knew she'd painted herself into a corner.

It was clear Harlan had Joanna right where he wanted her.

Chapter Nine

"SCALPEL, PLEASE, Watson," Harlan's voice was even and clipped. He didn't shout or hiss at Joanna in the operating room like he had the day before. Instead, he spoke his orders in a voice so calm and emotionless it was almost eerie. His eyes were completely without expression, his manner cold. Silently, Joanna almost wished the man would start screaming and swearing at her again just so she could reassure herself that he was human. Ever since her botched attempt at reverse psychology that morning, Harlan had become a virtual robot, using his frigid indifference towards her almost like a weapon. The man now seemed no more sexually interested in her than he would your average rock. It infuriated Joanna almost as much as it further inflamed her desire for him.

But she couldn't let him know that. Then he'd have even more power over her than he already did.

Joanna needed to get Harlan's attention in a way that would thrill and enthrall him, in a way that would throw him off guard and re-ignite his desire for her at the same time.

But how exactly could Joanna make that happen?

She had absolutely no idea.

"Scalpel, Watson!" Dr. Wilkinson's voice was raw with impatience. "*Now.*"

Joanna felt her cheeks flush with embarrassment as Dr. Wilkinson caught her daydreaming. "Scalpel, Dr. Wilkinson," she chirped as she palmed the instrument into his gloved hand.

There was a pause. Then—

"Goddamn it!" In a jerking reflex, Dr. Wilkinson flung the scalpel across the operating room and clutched his right hand, sharply sucking in his breath. Shirley Daniels, who was back on nurse-anesthetist duty, gasped.

"Sweet mother of Christ, Joanna," Harlan Wilkinson swore through gritted teeth. "What in God's name are you doing?" Harlan's unmasked forehead was twisting in pain as he clutched his right hand.

To her horror, Joanna saw that blood was seeping from the surgeon's right palm, soaking through the gloved fingers of his clutching left hand and forming a fast-growing puddle on the floor. Joanna realized that in her desire-fueled distraction, she must have handed Dr. Wilkinson the scalpel blade-first—the worst possible mistake any surgical nurse could make, ever. Nurses were fired – even had their licenses revoked – for less.

Well, she'd gotten his attention, all right. In absolutely the worst way possible.

"Oh, my God, Doctor—" Joanna stammered. "I-I'm so sorry. I-"

"Be quiet," Dr. Harlan Wilkinson hissed. He stamped his scrub-bootied foot onto a button embedded in the floor of the operating room that controlled an emergency intercom. "Code 15 in Operating Room Two. Code 15 in Operating Room Two. Send a relief team immediately."

Code 15.

At Covington Community Hospital, "Code 15" was the alert for "disabled surgeon." In a single careless moment, all of Joanna's years of nursing training and experience failed her, and she had rendered Dr. Harlan Wilkinson disabled.

And all because she was desperate for more sex.

Joanna felt the bottom fall out of her stomach. If the cut on Harlan's palm was deep enough, if it had severed a muscle, or even worse, a nerve—he might never operate on anyone again.

And it would be *her* fault.

"You're lucky this is routine elective surgery, Joanna," Harlan growled at her, his voice riddled with contempt. "If this had been the open-heart surgery scheduled for later today, you very well could have helped kill the patient with what you just did. Looks like all you managed to do this time around is destroy my career." Harlan held his bleeding right hand out away from the patient, a middle-aged woman seeking elective treatment for a troublesome but not life-threatening gall bladder problem. "Clamp the incision until the relief team gets here, Watson. *If* you think you can handle that."

Joanna obeyed, but it was all she could do to keep the surgical clamps steady. She was shaking all over. Harlan's rage-filled eyes stared at her from his spot across the operating table from her – a spot he was required by law to occupy, bleeding profusely or not – until the relief team arrived. Every moment that those eyes bore into her felt like a century. Joanna feared it would never end.

At long last, a bewildered third-year surgical resident and two young nurses appeared in the OR, already scrubbed and masked. "I'm injured," Dr. Wilkinson barked at them. "Take over. It's a standard gall-bladder removal, no complications other than the fact my fucking right hand is in ribbons. Plus, the whole surgical area is contaminated now. You'll need to re-sterilize everything and re-dress the surgery site."

With that, Harlan stomped out of the OR, almost slipping on the trail of blood left by his shredded right palm.

As soon as the new surgical team was in place, Joanna followed Harlan out of the OR into the scrub room, dreading what might happen next.

*****

Well, that was unexpected, Shirley Daniels thought to herself as she watched Dr. Harlan Wilkinson drag himself from the ER, bleeding like a stuck pig. She'd never seen anything like it in her entire career. Talk about cutting a man down a notch or two. Harlan had been cut down more than a notch—he'd been *cut down*, literally.

All of a sudden, the man didn't seem quite so McDreamy after all.

It was all Shirley could do to keep from laughing while she continued on with the operation under the new surgical team. To think—

just yesterday, the sight and sound of Dr. Harlan Wilkinson had been enough to make her panties damp. Now the man just made her mad.

What kind of crackpot surgeon lets his hand get sliced to ribbons on the job?

Maybe the kind of surgeon who has his mind on things other than the task at hand.

Namely, hot sex with his lead surgical nurse.

Shirley shook her head and chuckled despite herself as she manually adjusted one of the dials on the anesthesia machine. *Obviously, those two are in each other's pants,* she thought. And in all likelihood, it would end up with the both of them getting fired.

At one level, Shirley was jealous. Even if she thought Dr. Harlan Wilkinson was a crass, obnoxious jerk who made everyone who worked with him in the OR miserable, she still would have liked the opportunity to see him naked. The fact that the beautiful and sensual Joanna Watson beat her to it wasn't exactly surprising, either—but she still would have liked to have had the *opportunity* to try for it herself. Now that the man was probably permanently out of commission as far as performing surgery was concerned, Shirley wouldn't even have that. It was only a matter of time before he had to pull up stakes and head back north to Boston or New York or whatever Yankee city he was from, head dragging and tail between his legs.

Shirley wasn't usually the jealous type, but her roll in the hay with Jason the Super-Hot Frat Boy last night had exposed a side of herself she thought had been dead for a long time—her old *sorority girl* side.

And as anyone who's met a sorority girl or two knows, they are nothing if not vengeful, petty, and most of all, *competitive.*

As Shirley Daniels slowly turned down the amount of sodium pentothal flowing into the veins of the middle-aged woman lying on the operating table, she set about mentally devising a plan to get back at Joanna Watson for mucking things up for her in the bedroom department.

And Shirley thought she might as well start with Dr. Grenoway, the green third-year surgical resident who had just taken over for Dr. Wilkinson. He was young, spry—and if the uptight way he strutted around the hospital was any example—in desperate need of a good lay.

And the new-and-improved Shirley Daniels could take care of that in a flash.

If Shirley had her way, from now on *she* would be known as the most beautiful, sensual—and *available*—nurse around here—not Joanna Watson. No siree.

*****

Joanna held her breath as she stepped into the scrub room. Harlan was leaning over the scrub trough, his back to her as he washed and re-washed his right hand. The water ran red from his wound. Joanna's nursing skills told her the cut must be deep for it to still be bleeding so heavily.

Without a word, she went to the emergency first aid kit on the wall and took out sterile gauze pads and wrappings.

"Let me dress your wound for you, Doctor," she said, her voice shaking so much she could barely get the words out.

Harlan shut off the scrub taps with his left elbow and turned to face her. His face was blank, expressionless, his eyes vacant and dim. He held out his palm for her to see.

The cut went all the way to the bone.

"Don't bother, Watson. I'll need stitches, and you aren't qualified to do them on a palm cut this deep. Neither am I, actually. I'll need a hand surgeon to do it."

"We don't have any hand surgeons on staff at Covington, Doctor," she said, her voice barely above a whisper.

"I know." Dr. Harlan Wilkinson looked at the floor. The impact the injury might have on his career already weighed heavily on him, she could see that. In a few short minutes his physical presence had diminished from a powerful, virile surgeon to that of a frightened boy. Joanna could see the fear in his eyes as he stared at the deep, jagged incision in the middle of his otherwise perfect surgeon's hand.

Joanna took a deep breath and strengthened her resolve. She would have to help him, somehow. Helping him to survive his career-threatening injury was clearly the only avenue she had left inside Harlan's heart of stone, but she knew that after what she'd done, there was almost no chance at all he'd ever let her get anywhere close to his heart.

Still, she had to try. Even as he stood slump-shouldered in his injured, frightened state, both hands trembling, she felt an attraction to his body, mind, and soul that had just as much intensity as it had before—possibly even more so. Joanna could sense his weakness and vulnerability, and it made her pulse skitter with a strange mixture of compassion, anxiety, and excitement.

"Dr. Wilkinson, the nearest hand surgeon is in Raleigh-Durham, at the University of North Carolina Medical Center. If you'll let me dress your wound for the trip, I'll drive you there myself. It's the least I can do after what happened."

Harlan let out a heavy sigh, and slowly closed his eyes. "I would appreciate that, Joanna," he said. She took his wounded hand in her own, and found it cold and clammy. Still, even the touch of his damp, wounded hand against her still-gloved ones was enough to send a bolt of electricity all the way through her body.

A bolt of electricity that came to rest squarely between her legs, and stayed there. That moist heat slowly spread its radiating warmth out to the rest of her body as she dabbed antiseptic cream on Harlan's grievous wound. She applied pressure bandages, and finally wrapped his hand several times over with sterile gauze. She snipped the end of the roller bandage with hook scissors and secured the loose end with tape. Then she gently lowered Harlan's arm to his side, bending it at the elbow so his bandaged hand pointed towards the ceiling.

"You'll need to keep your hand elevated like this to help slow any additional bleeding," Joanna said, feeling stupid. Surely as a master surgeon, Harlan already knew that. But she had to keep talking, to keep saying *something*—or else she'd fall apart on the spot. "But it does look like you're finally getting some clotting, and the pressure bandages should also help. Do you feel lightheaded at all?"

"No."

"Are you sure?" Joanna asked. "You lost quite a bit of blood in there. You might even need a transfusion—"

"I'm fine." Harlan's gruff voice cut her off. "Just get me the hell out of here."

Chapter Ten

THE ROUTINE gall-bladder operation had proceeded uneventfully—well, uneventfully save for Dr. Wilkinson letting his right hand get shredded, anyway. Now that both he and his booty-call-slash-surgical-nurse Joanna Watson were both out of the way, Shirley Daniels could finally get down to business.

Shirley disconnected the patient from the anesthesia and prepped her for Recovery. All the while, she kept one eye on Dr. Grenoway's backside, which she could tell even through the baggy, bulky surgical scrubs was nice and tight. She couldn't wait to get her hands on it. And her newfound confidence told her it was only a matter of time before she did.

Once the patient was safely tucked into Recovery, Shirley followed Dr. Grenoway into the men's post-op locker room. He'd already discarded his scrubs into the hamper and was decontaminating in the steam shower.

It was technically against hospital regulations for nurses and doctors to be in the same locker room after an operation, but Shirley didn't care. And since Dr. Grenoway had been the only man in the OR, it wasn't as if she would be running into anybody else in there. If she had her way, Shirley knew that the post-op locker room was a perfect place for an impromptu tryst. Preferably standing up.

Shirley loosened her face mask and chuckled to herself. If only her parents knew just how naughty a girl she'd become. Hell, she might even tell them so herself—she was past due to visit them at the nursing home. Maybe she'd give them a glimpse of her new, sexually liberated self tonight when she brought them fresh sets of clean pajamas and a tuna-noodle casserole.

Hmph. Or maybe not.

Shirley didn't care what her parents—or anyone else, for that matter—thought about her newfound sensual self. All she did care about was satisfying the itch that needed scratching.

As she watched the shadow of Dr. Grenoway's lithe, muscular young body through the shower curtain, Shirley pondered exactly how she'd go about seducing him. Then she decided it was probably easiest just to jump in with both feet.

She shimmied off her scrubs, booties, and underwear until she stood naked in the chilly locker room. She grabbed a condom from her purse and tucked it between her teeth. Silently padding on bare feet to preserve the element of surprise, she tiptoed up to the shower stall and flung the curtain open in one swift motion, revealing herself to the younger doctor in all her naked glory. And the condom clutched in her mouth made her objective obvious.

He stared back at her, eyes wide and mouth agape. "What the-" he stammered, then trailed off. But even if his face looked shocked, his cock looked mighty happy to see her—it perked right up, literally, as soon as he laid eyes on her hot, naked body.

"That was some mighty nice operating you did in there, Dr. Grenoway," she cooed at him. "Now how about I do some operating of my own. On *you?*"

With that, she jumped into the shower stall with him, rubbing her naked body against his, which was slick with hot water and PhisoDerm.

Things were about to get steamy. And not from the shower, either.

Shirley clamped her mouth over Dr. Grenoway's gaping one and started a slow, deep tango with his tongue. At the same time, she began to run her palms up and down his rippled chest and abs, tracing intricate designs in the soapsuds on his skin with her fingertips.

Then she shoved him against the porcelain tile, braced herself against the wall, and wrapped one leg around his waist while she took him inside her She ground on him in perfect counterpoint to his thrusts, which came fast and urgent. After only a minute or two of frenzied lovemaking, Shirley vibrated in a wild climax, and the young doctor's own climax immediately followed. They collapsed into one another, breathing heavily under the steamy shower stream and reveling in the afterglow.

"What the hell was that for?" Dr. Grenoway breathed into Shirley's damp shoulder. "Not that I'm complaining or anything."

Shirley looked up at him and smiled. "Just for being you," she said. "By the way, Dr. Grenoway, what's your first name?"

"Dick," he said.

How appropriate, Shirley thought. "I hope you don't mind, Dick, but this was just a one-off thing. I'm not looking for a relationship right now."

Dick Grenoway looked relieved. "Good," he said. "Because if my fiancé found out about this, I'd be royally screwed."

"My lips are sealed," Shirley promised. And they were.

For now, at least. One never knew when that kind of information might come in handy.

Chapter Eleven

JOANNA AND Harlan were off to Raleigh-Durham in Joanna's battered old Honda.

They rode up Interstate 40 in silence. The car rattled along the highway on its worn-out shocks. She'd meant to buy a new car this year, but with all the legal bills from her divorce she hadn't been able to scrape the money together. The Honda embarrassed her— and not just because of how old and worn-out the car looked. All Joanna had to do was stare out through the windshield onto the hood to be reminded of her last wild tryst with Harlan.

And given what had just happened, the chance of her having another wild tryst with him across that car hood was next to nothing.

For the first forty miles of their drive, Harlan stared silently out the passenger window, never once glancing in Joanna's direction. He held his right arm up by the bent elbow to keep his injured hand above the level of his heart. In his heavy, forced silence, he seemed defeated—even small.

Joanna glanced away from the road and over at the sulking surgeon for a moment too long, and before she knew it, the old Honda clattered over a pothole. The entire car gave a heavy jerk.

"Ow!" Harlan hissed, clutching his injured hand to keep it from banging against the dashboard. "Doesn't this damn car have any shocks?"

"Sorry," Joanna replied in a small voice. "I've been meaning to replace them for a while, but my money's been very tight lately, and—"

Harlan scoffed. "Please. You're practically the best-paid nurse at Covington Community Hospital. And with all the overtime you put in, you should be swimming in cash."

Joanna had to force herself to keep her eyes on the road. "Pardon me, Doctor, but how exactly do you know how much money I make?"

"I looked it up. As chief of surgery I have access to payroll information whenever I want it."

"I see. But that doesn't mean you know anything about my financial situation, Doctor, which frankly is none of your business." Joanna was surprised at herself. An hour earlier she'd been grasping for some excuse – *any* excuse – to repair her shattered image in Harlan's eyes, and now she was back to being curt and defensive with him. Why? Joanna searched her mind for an answer, but could find none.

Except maybe the fact that she *enjoyed* arguing with this man.

Harlan was silent for a few minutes. The only sound was the whooshing vibration of the Honda's tires against the asphalt. After a long pause, he spoke. "Joanna, I don't mean to pry, but if you're having some financial problems—"

"You *are* prying," Joanna's tone was sharp, but inside she was secretly thrilled that he was taking personal interest in her again. "If you don't mind me saying so, Doctor—"

"Please, call me Harlan," he interrupted.

Joanna kept her face pointed straight at the road so Harlan couldn't see her smile. "All right, *Harlan*. What business is it of yours that I'm broke?"

"You're broke?"

Joanna bit her tongue. Already, she had revealed too much. She was as inept at male-female relations as ever. "Well, not *broke*, exactly. Just – just in a tight position, is all."

"I see. And given your income, how exactly is that possible?"

Joanna didn't answer. She glanced over her shoulder to check her blind spot before changing lanes.

Harlan wasn't taking her silence lightly. "Joanna, I asked you a question."

"And I already told you it was none of your damn business." Joanna merged the Honda into the exit lane.

Harlan heaved a heavy sigh. "Joanna, it's obvious that this accident happened"—Harlan gestured with his bandaged hand—"because you were distracted by something. If one of my nurses is distracted in the OR, I want to know *why*. I'm asking you this question strictly for professional reasons."

Joanna's heart sank. *Strictly for professional reasons.* That meant Harlan Wilkinson cared nothing for her personally.

And she wasn't about to confess that she'd been distracted in the OR because she was desperate for sex – and not because she was broke. "I would still prefer not to talk about it," she finally said, her voice tight and squeaky.

"Fine," Harlan snapped. "But given what you did to me, Joanna, at some point I would appreciate an explanation as to what might cause a nurse of your considerable skill and experience to make that kind of a mistake. You owe me that, at least."

Joanna didn't answer. She braked the car to take the steep curve of the merge ramp onto I-340. They rode on in silence for the next six miles, until Joanna adjusted the car's speed to meet the slower pace of city traffic. She scanned the green-and-white highway signs for the correct exit. They would be at University Hospital in a matter of minutes.

"So is this hand surgeon you're taking me to any good, Joanna?"

Joanna swallowed a few times before answering. Her mouth had gone cotton-dry, and she was getting a splitting headache. She tightened her grip on the steering wheel. "Yes, he's very, very good. Dr. Larry Rosenbaum's his name. He and Dr. Turnblatt were very good friends. Dr. Turnblatt referred a lot of patients to him."

"Does a little hospital like Covington see a lot of severe hand injuries, then?" Harlan posed the question politely, but she could still hear animosity in his voice.

"Oh yes. More than you might think. Many of the hand injuries we get are farming-related. Most of them are treatable in the emergency room, but the more serious ones – the ones where someone has gotten his hand caught in a thresher or something – require surgery. Covington's never had the resources to afford having a full-time hand surgeon on staff, so Dr. Turnblatt would just do what he could to stabilize those patients and then send them up the road to Dr. Rosenblum."

"Uh huh," was Harlan's dismissive reply. Joanna cut her eyes in his direction and saw he was staring intently at his bandaged right hand, as if he could scarcely believe the sight of it. The knowledge that one careless act on her part could potentially destroy this obviously brilliant man's entire career tore at her insides – the same insides that were still aflame with heady desire for him.

Joanna blinked back tears as she pulled her car off the freeway and onto the city street that dead-ended into University Hospital's main parking garage. She wouldn't show him a moment's weakness—she *wouldn't*. Joanna knew that she needed to show Harlan Wilkinson just how much strength she possessed. Perhaps, just perhaps, her show of strength in probably the most frightening, uncertain time in Harlan's life would be the way into his heart. . . .

"Joanna, what the hell are you doing?" Harlan shouted, and grabbed hold of the steering wheel with his left hand, turning it sharply to keep the car from ramming straight into a streetlight. Joanna shuddered as she realized that she had been so lost in lust for Harlan Wilkinson that she'd very nearly crashed the car.

What on earth was this man doing to her?

Joanna took several deep cleansing breaths in a futile effort to calm herself down. Now running on pure adrenaline, she somehow managed to pull the car into the University Hospital parking garage and to secure a parking space. She brought the car to a stop, and as soon as she pulled the key from the ignition, against her will, her head laid itself down on the steering wheel. The conflicting emotions racking her body were fast becoming too much for her to handle. Joanna squeezed her eyes shut and stiffened her throat muscles to keep from sobbing out loud.

Joanna felt a hand on her shoulder. A strong, masculine hand that still carried a soft, gentle touch. The feel of Harlan's hand on her body was enough to stir her entire being. She could feel the waves of his sexual magnetism wending their way through his fingers and into her skin, making her entire body pulse with anticipation. The prolonged buildup of her desire for this man was fast becoming unbearable.

Something had to give, and soon.

Joanna looked up and her green eyes met Harlan's pale blue ones, which peered at her with deep intensity. Her stomach did a flip-flop, and she had to break off her gaze from his to keep from losing control.

"Joanna?" Harlan's voice was soft with concern. "Are you all right?"

Joanna swallowed hard, took a deep breath, and replied "Yes. I—I'm sorry, I guess I'm a little shook up, is all. I've never lost control of my car before. Hell, I've never lost control of *anything* before—"

"We all have our bad days," Harlan said. "Take me to this damn hand surgeon, will you? I need to see if I have a career left."

With that, Harlan stepped out of the car and headed for the parking garage elevator.

Chapter Twelve

JOANNA SAT in a molded plastic chair in Dr. Larry Rosenblum's waiting room, flipping through a tattered copy of *Life & Style* with one hand, and biting her nails down to the quick on the other. She stared at the glossy paparazzi photographs of Jennifer Aniston and Britney Spears until her eyes glazed over, and when that happened, she glanced up at the waiting-room clock for the umpteenth time.

Dr. Rosenblum had rearranged his afternoon surgery schedule to fit in an examination of Harlan's wound. Joanna knew he had done so in respect for the sacred surgeons' brotherhood, since he refused to take any money for the job. He might even get to write a research article about it, since deep scalpel wounds of surgeons' hands weren't exactly common.

Harlan had been in Dr. Rosenblum's examination room for almost an hour. Joanna had no idea what could be taking so long, unless the two surgeons had fallen into swapping war stories or talking baseball. Just as Joanna was starting to re-read for the eighth or ninth time a six-month-old article on why Jennifer Aniston's relationship with John Mayer was doomed to failure, a shout in the next room startled her.

"How DARE you imply that—" Harlan's voice boomed. She tried to make out the rest, but part of the shouts were drowned out by the air conditioning.

"Goddamn you! God*DAMN* you!"

Joanna chuckled to herself. *I suppose that means they're not talking baseball*, she thought.

Harlan Wilkinson burst into the waiting room, which thankfully was empty save for Joanna. She noticed his right hand was now un-bandaged save for a light gauze dressing. Dr. Rosenblum had closed the cut on his palm with nine perfectly executed butterfly stitches.

"I don't know what kind of substandard, incompetent *numbskull* you've brought me all this way to see, Joanna, but we are leaving. *Now*."

A split second later, Dr. Larry Rosenblum, a gentle-voiced, balding Jewish man in his late sixties, followed Harlan out into the waiting room. "Dr. Wilkinson, wait. Please. We need to talk about your next course of treatment—"

"My next course of treatment will be getting the hell away from you." With that charming remark, Harlan Wilkinson grabbed his jacket off Dr. Rosenblum's brass coat tree and stomped out into the hall, slamming the office door behind him with a crash.

Joanna didn't know what to think. She had known and respected Dr. Rosenblum for years, and was mortified by Harlan's crass behavior towards him.

She was even more mortified by the fact that Harlan's crass behavior thrilled and aroused her more than anything she had ever witnessed.

For reasons Joanna still couldn't begin to understand, her heart was pounding in her ears at the echoes of Harlan's booming baritone, her stomach fluttering as her body reverberated with each and every vibration his stomping feet made in the linoleum.

Joanna took a moment to collect herself and then stepped over to face the kindly old surgeon she and Dr. Turnblatt had known and worked with for so many years. "I'm sorry, Larry. Had I known he would behave like this, I—"

Dr. Rosenblum held up his hand. "It's all right, Joanna. This is exactly how I would expect a surgeon of his reputation to react when I told him what I did."

"React? React to what?"

Larry Rosenblum, MD, a hand surgeon with a medical degree from Duke and more than thirty years' experience in his highly specialized field, motioned for Joanna to sit down. She did.

"Joanna, can you tell me exactly what you think happened when Dr. Wilkinson dropped the scalpel in the OR and got cut?"

Joanna flushed and looked at the floor. "I handed him the scalpel blade-first, Larry. It was my mistake—"

Dr. Rosenblum's eyebrows raised. "Are you absolutely sure about that?"

Joanna bit her lip. No, she wasn't *absolutely* sure. But she *had* been daydreaming – not to mention so distracted by Harlan's sex appeal she wasn't concentrating on the task at hand. So there couldn't possibly be any other explanation for the accident. Could there?

"Joanna, I've inspected Dr. Wilkinson's wound very carefully, and I've determined that the accident was his own fault. You handed him the scalpel properly. He just dropped it, and the blade cut him on its way down."

"But—but that's impossible!" Joanna cried. She couldn't fathom Harlan making that kind of mistake.

"I'm afraid not, Joanna," Dr. Rosenblum plopped into the plastic chair next to her own and sighed. "The shape and direction of the cut makes it clear that it occurred from him not having a good grip on the scalpel when he took it from you, causing it to slip. Had you handed it to him blade-first, like you thought, the cut would have been perfectly smooth and straight, and likely the exact length of the scalpel blade. That's just not the case here. These kinds of surgery-related hand injuries don't happen that often, but when they do, they are almost always the surgeon's fault."

Joanna was dumbstruck. "Are you sure?"

Dr. Rosenblum nodded. "I've been called upon to consult on cases of this kind in several lawsuits, and that's just been the consistent finding when I see jagged palm cuts like this. It looks to me like Dr. Wilkinson was just plain careless. And I told him as much."

Joanna was stunned. The very idea of Harlan being "just plain careless" just didn't make sense. What's more, it showed Joanna that Harlan, was, like her, an imperfect, fallible human being – something that he might not be willing to admit to himself.

"I guess he didn't take the news very well," Joanna said.

"Well, as I'm sure you already know, Joanna, surgeons often like to think of themselves as superhuman. Most surgeons aren't known for accepting even constructive criticism, let alone reminders that they can make careless mistakes. But I think in this case, it's pretty clear that's exactly what Dr. Wilkinson did."

Joanna got up and pulled her jacket off the brass coat tree. "I suppose I should get going. I'm Dr. Wilkinson's ride home, and—"

"I suggest you take the man out for a stiff drink or two," Dr. Rosenblum said, helping Joanna into her jacket like a true Southern gentleman. "He'll need it, especially after I file my report with your hospital's administration."

Joanna stopped short. "Report? What do you mean?"

Dr. Rosenblum shook his head, sadly. "By order of state law, I am required to make a report to Covington Hospital's administration of my clinical opinion as to why a scalpel injury of this nature occurred in their OR. I plan to tell them the truth. I'm afraid it could mean some serious consequences for Dr. Wilkinson."

"What kind of consequences, exactly?"

Dr. Rosenblum shook his head again. "That's at the discretion of the hospital, as well as the state medical board. At best he could be fined, at worst he could have his medical license revoked. I suspect he'll get something in between."

"Like what?" Joanna's voice was trembling now.

"Likely he'll get placed on unpaid leave for a month or two."

"But they can't do that! He's only just started! He's-" Joanna blurted. She stopped short, took a moment to compose herself. She couldn't fall apart now. Not in front of Dr. Rosenblum. Not with so much at stake.

Dr. Rosenblum placed a firm hand on her shoulder. "Joanna, I think the best thing you can do for Dr.Wilkinson right now is to help him relax. Take him out for a drink, buy him dinner, have a nice conversation with him that doesn't have anything to do with surgery. He could just use a good friend right now, and I've known you long enough to understand that being a good friend is something you excel at."

Joanna smiled, hugged the kindly old surgeon, and left.

No matter what Dr. Rosenblum might think of her, she didn't share his confidence in her ability to be just a good friend to Dr. Harlan Wilkinson. Not one bit.

Sex had a nasty habit of getting in the way of friendship.

Chapter Thirteen

HARLAN STARED at Joanna from across a table at La Colatta, a small Italian restaurant in downtown Raleigh. La Colatta had been a favorite of hers for many years – she and Dr. Turnblatt often had lunch here together when she accompanied him on surgical field trip demonstrations at University Hospital.

A harried waitress had just set down a basket of fresh-baked rolls and two glasses of ice water for them to pick at until she could have time to take their order. But instead of deciding what he wanted to eat, Harlan grabbed one of the warm rolls and started shredding it into small pieces with the nimble fingers of his left hand. Joanna squirmed in her seat, imagining what it would feel like to have those fingers on her again. She grabbed a roll for herself and smothered it in butter in a vain effort to distract herself.

"All that butter's bad for your health," Harlan said, dismembering yet another roll. "Not to mention your figure."

"Oh, I don't know," Joanna retorted. "I've never had a problem staying healthy, what with all the running around I have to do for you arrogant surgeon types all the time. Thanks to that, I'm the same size now as I was when I was eighteen."

Harlan dusted crumbs off the fingers of his left hand. His now stitched-up right one hovered down at his side. "And how old are you now, Joanna?"

"Thirty-six."

Harlan didn't comment further. He just shrugged and then pretended to be interested in the menu.

"So, what are you going to order?" Joanna asked. "The stuffed shells are very good here, by the way. And so's the veal. Don't worry about the price, it's my treat."

Harlan glanced up at Joanna over the edge of his menu, shrugged, and said nothing.

"I also recommend the spaghetti Bolognese, if you're looking for something heavier," Joanna chirped. "It's the specialty of the house."

"Hmm," was Harlan's noncommittal reply. A series of nervous tics jerked along his hard, angular jaw line. Joanna hoped the tics were a sign of sexual tension on his part, but somehow she doubted it.

"How about I order a nice Chianti for us?" Joanna offered, hoping to break the tension. "I'll get you the best one on the menu."

Harlan set his menu down, his eyes and expression getting more steely by the second. "Don't worry about the price, huh? Expensive Chianti, too? Funny, Joanna, earlier today I thought you said you were broke."

Joanna took a sip from her water glass. "I am a little broke, but don't worry. That's why God invented MasterCard."

Harlan rolled his eyes at this.

The waitress finally appeared. Joanna ordered the stuffed shells, a green salad, and a calamari appetizer. At Joanna's recommendation Harlan ordered the spaghetti Bolognese, which pleased her. Then he tossed his menu gruffly at the waitress and ordered a gin and tonic, which did not please her at all. The waitress dashed off for the kitchen before Joanna could protest or even order a glass of wine of her own.

"Gin and tonic? What about Chianti? We're at an Italian restaurant. We should have a good Chianti."

Harlan cleared his throat. "I hate Chianti. I hate all wine, in fact."

Joanna's heart sank. She'd never heard of anyone—let alone someone as well educated and sophisticated at Harlan—hating wine. "Why is that?"

"Gives me a headache. Plus, you can get drunk a helluva lot faster on hard liquor. You really should try it sometime." Harlan's mood was as black as pitch, and getting blacker by the second. Joanna knew she had to do something to lighten the man up, or else this would be one unbearable meal. Not to mention the fact that the darker the man's mood got, the less chance she had of getting his pants off again.

"No, thank you, Harlan. I prefer to be as sober as possible when I'm eating Italian food. Otherwise, I'll get too messy and sloppy with my eating, and when I do that, all the tomato sauce tends to get into some unmentionable places." Joanna added a flirty toss of her hair – a trademark Southern belle move if there ever was one – and smiled.

The left corner of Harlan's frowning mouth tipped upward ever so slightly. Maybe there was hope for her sex life after all. It was a start. Who knew – if she could manage to keep cracking suggestive jokes, she might even manage to melt the man's heart a little.

Harlan's gin and tonic arrived. He downed it in one gulp and ordered another. Joanna timidly asked the waitress to bring her a glass of moderately-priced Merlot. Harlan attacked the fresh drink shortly after the waitress brought it, while Joanna only sipped her Merlot.

If Harlan kept hitting the bottle this hard, he just might soften up. *Maybe there's still a chance for me to get lucky tonight*, she thought.

"So, what do you think of North Carolina?" Joanna finally asked, eyeing the level of liquid left in Harlan's second highball in as many minutes. "How does it compare to Boston?"

"There's no comparison. No comparison at all." Harlan ran his left index finger around and around the rim of his highball glass in a way that Joanna found insanely erotic. She felt her body starting to tingle.

"No comparison at all?" she asked, shifting a little in her seat. Her nurse's uniform slacks suddenly felt itchy, even too tight. "Do you mean that in a good way or a bad way?"

Harlan polished off the rest of his second gin and tonic and then leaned back in his chair, stretching out his arms and then cupping the fingers of his left hand behind his head. He kept his injured right hand on the table, right next to his empty highball glass. "Both," he said.

"What do you mean?"

Harlan sighed loudly and then settled back into a regular sitting position. Joanna could tell by his fluid movements and more relaxed posture that the alcohol was already working on him, and working well. "I mean," he said, fiddling with his red cloth napkin, "that there are things about North Carolina that I absolutely love – like the beautiful scenery, the fresh air, the friendly people. And then there are things that I absolutely hate."

Joanna took another sip of wine. "Such as?"

"I'd prefer not to talk about the things I hate tonight." Joanna saw the nervous tics pulling at Harlan's jaw line again, although they weren't as deep this time. "I've had enough bad will for one day." Harlan crumpled his napkin into a ball and sighed again.

Joanna stared thoughtfully into her wine glass for a moment, pondering whether or not it was safe to tread too close to the topic of Harlan's injury. She decided to approach it with caution. "Did Dr. Rosenblum think your injury is bad enough to affect your surgical career at all?" Joanna hoped the injury wasn't permanent.

"I think your Dr. Rosenblum is full of crap, frankly."

"No, he's not," Joanna retorted. "He's very respected. He's one of the best hand surgeons on the East Coast, Harlan."

Harlan scoffed. "If he really were any good, he'd be in Boston or New York."

Joanna was deeply offended by Harlan's not-so-subtle potshot at her home state, but she made no show of it in her face. She would match him, tit for tat. "Oh? Then tell me something, Harlan. If you think North Carolina so crummy, what are *you* doing practicing here?"

Harlan laughed, but it wasn't a genuine laugh. It was forced, almost metallic. "You really are one tough lady, Joanna Watson," he said. "You just don't let up, do you?" Harlan frowned and rubbed at his eyes with his good hand. Joanna could tell that she had touched a nerve. The tiniest speck of vulnerability had arisen in Harlan's rugged features.

Joanna felt things heat up down south.

"Well?" Joanna prodded. "Are you going to tell me why you moved here or not?"

"That's kind of a long story," Harlan finally said, just as their calamari appetizer arrived.

Joanna dove right into the pile of fried squid. "Well, we do seem to have plenty of time. We're both off surgery duty until further notice, after all."

Harlan frowned. "So?"

"So tell me the long story."

Harlan sucked at the dregs of his gin and tonic and gave Joanna a black look capable of melting iron. "No."

Joanna met his fierce gaze without flinching. She knew it was time for her to dig deeper. Much deeper. "Dr. Rosenblum told me that it's your own damn fault you got cut," she snapped.

Harlan's lips thinned with irritation, but he said nothing.

"Dr. Rosenblum said you made a careless mistake, Harlan," she went on. "Is that true?"

"I'm not going to answer that," Harlan snarled, and then flagged down the waitress for another drink.

"Why not?"

"Because I'm not," he replied, and to Joanna's shock, he put his head in his hands, covering his face completely. He finally looked up, and gave her a hard look. "I'm a failure, Joanna. That's why I'm in North Carolina now, and not Boston. There, I said it. Are you happy now?"

"You're not a failure, Harlan. You just made a mistake, that's all. We all do."

Harlan gestured with his injured right hand. "I'm not talking about what happened today. I'm talking about my life in general.

I'm a failure, Joanna. I'm here in North Carolina because of something that happened to me on my last Doctors Without Borders excursion, among other things. Things that pretty much render me incapable of ever working in a first-class hospital ever again."

Joanna reached across the table and put her right hand over Harlan's left one. The feel of his skin on hers was exciting, startling, and sensual all at the same time. Involuntarily, Joanna sucked in her breath as a hot surge of electricity jolted up her arm, ran through her neck and chest, and landed squarely between her legs. She took a deep breath to cool herself, and focused her eyes back on Harlan's brooding ones before speaking. "Harlan, I don't know what you could have possibly done to think you're a failure. You're a confident, capable, and obviously gifted man. I've thought so almost from the moment I met you."

Harlan's sandy blond eyebrows knitted. "Funny, it seemed to me you thought I was a total asshole when we first met."

Joanna had to laugh. She squeezed his hand, and to her surprise and delight, he squeezed hers back. "Actually, yes, I did. But even assholes can be confident, capable, and gifted. The two things aren't mutually exclusive."

To her amazement, Joanna found she was actually getting through to Harlan. After so many days of playing the super-tough, ultra-masculine surgeon, he was letting his guard down with her a little. Perhaps, just perhaps, it wouldn't be as hard for her to win his love as she thought.

Harlan squeezed her hand again, harder this time. "Joanna, I owe you an apology."

"Oh, really? Why?"

The waitress arrived with Harlan's third gin and tonic. He caressed the sweating highball glass with his fingers but didn't take a drink. "I think you know why, Joanna. I wrongly accused you of cutting me in the OR. I manipulated you into thinking the accident was your fault, when it wasn't. I—" Harlan trailed off and stared into his highball glass.

"Go on."

After a long pause Harlan took another cautious sip of his third gin and tonic of the evening. Even with that much alcohol in his system, the necessary words were not coming easily to him. Joanna squeezed his hand again, and this time, his fingers caressed the inside of her hand by way of responding. The feel of his smooth, ministering fingertips on her skin was electric.

"The truth is, Joanna, I've been making careless mistakes in my surgical practice for years now. What happened today was just the first mistake that physically injured someone. Despite all the mistakes I've made before, I didn't want to accept that I was capable of being so inept at my own job, so I blamed you instead. Then when Dr. Rosenblum saw through me – well, I guess I just lost it. I'm sorry."

Harlan sighed and hung his head. Joanna could feel from the sadness and tension in his fingers as they gripped hers.

"I suppose it's a mixed blessing that the person I injured was myself, instead of you or my patient," Harlan went on. Joanna could smell the alcohol on his breath now. It mixed with the scent of his aftershave and his own distinctive, musky male scent to form a malleable, almost acid-like odor that she supposed was the scent of fear. Her heart went out to him.

"But I'm afraid that if there's a next time, I won't be so lucky," he said. Harlan let go of Joanna's hand and started fiddling with his napkin again. He didn't touch the calamari, so Joanna polished the rest of it off herself.

Licking some excess grease off her fingers, Joanna gave Harlan a gentle smile, which seemed to relax him a little. "Thank you for the apology, Harlan. I appreciate it, I really do. But it seems that there's a lot more to this than what you're telling me."

Harlan's jaw line hardened, erupting into dozens of nervous tics again. "I don't know what you mean. I just spilled my guts to you—"

"The other mistakes, Harlan. What other careless mistakes have you made in your career? In your life?"

"I don't want to talk about this any more, Joanna."

"But—

Harlan put up his hand. His *right* hand, palm first. Joanna studied the nine perfect butterfly stitches on his palm for a moment. She started to speak, but Harlan cut her off.

"This—" Harlan indicated his wound. "is not your fault, Joanna. It was *my* fault. A lot of other things are my fault, too, but I'm not going to discuss those things with you. Not tonight, not ever. Do you understand?"

"Harlan, just tell me—"

"Joanna, please just leave me alone!" Harlan slammed his left palm on the tabletop, hard. The water glasses shook, and his half-empty highball glass tipped over, spilling liquor everywhere. A few of La Colatta's other customers turned to stare.

Joanna was dumbstruck. She felt her cheeks color, and her insides, which just moments ago had been aflame with desire, went stone cold. "Excuse me," she whispered, a lump fast forming in her throat as she sped off for the ladies' room.

*****

Joanna stood at the sink in La Colatta's tiny ladies' room. Someone knocked on the locked door of the single-toilet bathroom hoping to use it, but Joanna wasn't quite ready to leave yet.

Joanna washed and re-washed her hands under the ice-cold taps. She felt the urgent need to wash off all traces of Harlan Wilkinson's touch. The man evoked such strong feelings of arousal in her that she feared she lose control of herself and drop her drawers right in the middle of the restaurant if she didn't cool off.

And of course there was the little problem of Harlan being cold as ice himself at the moment. She wasn't optimistic of her chances of seducing him again.

Harlan harbored more than a few demons in his psyche – that was clear. But more and more, Joanna got the feeling that she didn't want to know what those demons were. Even as she had succeeded somewhat at poking underneath Harlan's hard exterior to expose the vulnerable, terrified little boy underneath – if only for a moment—Joanna was afraid to probe him any further. She was afraid if she did, she'd lose any chance she had with him entirely.

On the other hand, Joanna figured she didn't stand a chance with him at all so long as the real Harlan Wilkinson stayed buried underneath that impenetrable façade he'd built up around himself, either.

Well, she was damned if she did and damned if she didn't. She just couldn't win.

Joanna dried her hands on the old-fashioned roller towel, and gazed at her reflection in the mirror. At thirty-six, she was still a very attractive woman. The physical activity of a hospital nurse's job kept her fit, and she also enjoyed running and hiking on the local mountain trails when she had time. She'd always been shy of the sun and had never smoked, so her complexion was smooth, without even the slightest hint of crow's feet or laugh lines. She'd never had any gray hair or felt the need to color her naturally straight, strawberry-blond tresses, which she always wore in a simple half-ponytail pulled back from her face. Her breasts were small but firm, and didn't sag like those of many women her age. Her hips were slight, but just curvy enough for her petite frame.

Joanna sighed at her reflection. She was a desirable woman, and she knew it. Why on earth had she only had sex with two men—her fumbling ex-husband and the overwrought, emotionally unstable Harlan Wilkinson? And why was she wasting her time on Dr. Harlan Wilkinson when she could probably have any single man she wanted?

Probably because Dr. Harlan Wilkinson was the first man who had ever made her feel like a complete woman, that's why.

Even if the man did carry some serious emotional baggage, Joanna couldn't walk away from him. It had taken thirty-six years for her to experience the kind of pleasure that Harlan brought out of the deepest, darkest recesses of her body. If she lost him now, Joanna was afraid she'd never experience that kind of pleasure again.

She had to make this work. She *had* to.

Joanna shouldered her purse and left the bathroom, nodding her apologies to the line of impatient women waiting to use the facilities. She marched back into the restaurant, prepared to make Harlan hers once and for all.

But when she got back to their table, Harlan was gone.

Chapter Fourteen

JOANNA STARED at her untouched stuffed-shell entrée, humiliated. Harlan's jacket was gone from the back of his chair, and his own entrée was missing. When Joanna asked the overworked waitress if she had seen where her dinner companion had gone, the girl explained that Harlan had requested a takeout box for his spaghetti Bolognese and left the restaurant while Joanna was still in the bathroom.

He probably went to a bar, Joanna seethed. *I guess three gin and tonics weren't enough for him.* She picked at her salad and pasta dish but found that her appetite had completely disappeared. She flagged down the waitress for a takeout box and the check. The waitress returned with a Styrofoam takeout box, but told her the bill had already been paid in full "by the gentleman who just left."

Well, the "gentleman who just left" could find his own goddamn ride back to Statesville. What an ill-mannered, selfish Yankee jerk. That was it. Even if he was the only man who had ever brought her to ecstasy, Joanna was through with him. Absolutely through.

She gathered her things and headed out to her car. She searched the windshield to see if Harlan might have had the common courtesy to leave her a note, but of course he had not. With a sigh of defeat, Joanna unlocked her car door, got in, and tossed her shoulder bag onto the passenger seat. Just as she keyed the ignition, her cell phone rang.

She fished it out of her shoulder bag. "Hello?"

"Joanna, it's Maryam Malone. Where are you? And where's Dr. Wilkinson?"

"I'm in Raleigh. I brought Dr. Wilkinson here to see Dr. Rosenblum, about his hand injury. You heard about the accident in the OR, I assume?"

Maryam clucked. "Yes, I did. So Darth Vader got cut, huh? I'll bet that wasn't a pretty sight."

Joanna laughed in spite of herself. "You have no idea."

"I assume he's still with you, then?" The old nurse sounded frazzled. Joanna figured Maryam must be pulling double-duty since Joanna had left with Harlan earlier in the day.

"No, actually he's not."

"I see," The older woman sounded surprised. "So where is he now?"

Joanna bit her lip before answering. "Well, you see Maryam, I don't exactly know."

"What do you mean? I thought you drove him to Raleigh yourself."

"I did."

Maryam sighed on her end of the line. "So, where is he?"

"I don't know. We were having dinner, and he took off when I was in the bathroom."

"You were having dinner with him, Joanna? You actually sat down to dinner with Darth Vader himself?" Maryam sounded both surprised and amused.

"I only did it at Larry Rosenblum's suggestion. He seemed to think Dr. Wilkinson would need to do some relaxing after the bad news Larry gave him." Joanna wasn't sure how much of that bad news she should reveal to her friend and colleague. Although she respected the older nurse very much, Joanna had learned the hard way over the years that Maryam was also a bit of a gossip.

And Maryam's busybody tendencies were certainly on display today. "What bad news is that, Joanna?" the older woman gushed, anxious. "Everyone here is *dying* to know what really happened. Word around the ward right now is you handed him the scalpel wrong, but I'm having a hard time believing that."

"Well—"

"It wasn't your fault, was it? I hope not. I really can't stand to lose another nurse right now." Maryam sounded genuinely concerned for Joanna.

"*Another* nurse? What do you mean?"

"Lindsay Strouse just handed in her notice. She's taking a job at St. Michael's, the Catholic hospital in Durham. She only gave me a week's notice, too. And Shirley Daniels is threatening to quit too if Darth Vader doesn't shape up his OR behavior."

Joanna clucked. "That's odd. Shirley usually isn't one to complain publicly about anything."

"I know," Maryam said. "Something's gotten into Shirley lately. She's changed."

I'll say, Joanna thought to herself. *And I bet I know why.*

"I don't know what's going on with Shirley Daniels," Maryam went on, "but I hope to God *she* doesn't quit too, because I don't know where I'm supposed to find a surgery / recovery nurse *and* a nurse-anesthetist in the same week in the middle of North Carolina. Do you think you could talk the both of them into staying?"

"I'll try," Joanna said, noncommittal.

"Joanna?" Maryam pleaded. "You aren't being fired for this, are you?"

"Don't worry, Maryam," Joanna finally replied. "Larry Rosenblum inspected the wound and determined it was Dr. Wilkinson's own fault, so the hospital can't do anything to me. I'll be sticking around for a while."

Maryam guffawed. "You mean to tell me that Darth Vader cut his *own* hand? Well, then *he'll* be fired for sure." Maryam laughed again, harder this time. Joanna thought she heard the older woman slapping her knee.

Joanna didn't join in Maryam's laughter. Even after his callous treatment of her in the restaurant, she still couldn't bring herself to have a laugh at Harlan's expense.

"Joanna, are you there?"

"Yes," she answered, her voice clipped. "Look, Maryam, is there something I can do for you? If so, make it quick. I've got to get back on the road."

Maryam sighed. "Well, I just called to tell you Administration has ordered that you take at least the rest of the week off until they could figure out what happened for sure in the OR today. But it looks like given what Dr. Rosenblum found out you won't need to be off quite that long. Even if you do come back after a day or two, I'll still be really short-staffed in the meantime. So if you can find it in your heart to try to recruit some more nurses for me – anyone you might know from your school days or whatever – I would be eternally grateful."

Joanna sighed. She knew that not one of her old nursing-school chums would consider a low-paying job at a rural hospital, but she couldn't bring herself to give Maryam that bad news. "I'll see what I can do. And Maryam, I would really appreciate it if you would keep what I told you about Harlan's accident to yourself. The truth will come out eventually, since Larry Rosenblum's filing his report with Administration, and I'd prefer it came out through the proper channels."

"My lips are sealed," Maryam replied, and broke the connection.

Joanna hoped Maryam kept her word, but she wasn't holding her breath.

*****

As Joanna made the two-hour drive back to Statesville alone, a hundred troubling thoughts crossed her mind. What if something had happened to Harlan in Raleigh? What if he'd been mugged, or hit by a city bus, or passed out drunk in the gutter? Would it be her fault? What if he reported her to Administration for abandoning him in town?

At the last thought, Joanna laughed out loud. "Abandoning" him? How could she think such a thing? After all, *he* had ditched *her.*

Still, Harlan's treatment of her stung. It was the only time in her life a man had ever walked away from her. Even with her irritating ex-husband Bob, *she* had been the one to do the leaving, and that was only after she was fed up with almost ten years of marital misery. To think, just a few hours ago she had been intent on seducing Harlan—and instead she'd gotten ditched in a public place.

The familiar landmarks of the long Raleigh-Statesville drive passed her one by one. Billboards for Howard's Truck Stop and Truck Wash, Carolina Antique Market, and The Cherokee Gift Emporium. The faded sign marking the turnoff to the scenic Blue Ridge Parkway, and many of the typical brown highway signs advertising state parks and campgrounds all passed her by. One of those brown highway signs caught her eye – "Carl Sandburg National Historic Site: Next Right, 25 mi."

Joanna glanced at her watch. It was already after six, which meant the national park affiliated with the famous poet's home was probably closed for the day. But she'd always heard the views and vistas near the famous landmark were lovely, especially in the early springtime when the wild rhododendrons were in bloom. And after the day's events, she could use a few moments' respite in a calm, beautiful place. She decided to make a brief detour onto Highway 225 and head towards the Carl Sandburg Home, maybe pull off at one of the many scenic overlooks along the way. She'd heard there were many mountain waterfalls in the vicinity – perhaps she would find one, even drink from its pure mountain water as she had done from the springs her father used to take her on hikes to find when she was a little girl.

Joanna eased the rattling old Honda onto the exit ramp that merged with the old, winding two-lane highway that led into the Blue Ridge mountain hideaways where Sandburg, the famous poet, had once found such inspiration.

After driving for about twenty-five minutes, she saw more signs. "Now Entering Pisgah National Forest." "Elk Falls Trail, Next Right."

On a whim, she followed the Elk Falls Trail sign onto a narrow gravel road that led straight into hemlock forest. After following the rough, rutted road for almost a mile, she came into a small parking lot. There was a single sign reading "Elk Falls Trailhead," a couple of Porta-Potties, and a trash can, but no other cars. There wasn't another soul in sight.

Good, she thought. A perfect spot for some time alone.

Joanna figured she'd be safe to hike the trail alone until sunset, which gave her about and hour and a half. She kept a pair of sturdy hiking boots in her trunk, and her nurse's attire was comfortable. If she reached the waterfall in time it would be ideal, but if not, at least the fresh mountain air and the sight of the first leaves of springtime would be calming.

Joanna parked the car in one of the empty spots. She was excited at the prospect of a nice long hike in the woods, but she was even more excited at the prospect of something else.

She wasn't going to pull the hiking boots out of her trunk just yet. She had something to do first.

Joanna's fingers strayed to the waistband of her nurse's scrubs. In her excitement she fumbled with the drawstring waist, but soon she had her scrub bottoms and panties down. She reached between her legs, giving herself the much-needed relief from the tension that had been building in her body all day long.

Joanna rearranged her clothing and got out of the car. She pulled her hiking boots out of the trunk, along with the flashlight, hat, and walking stick she always kept there. Once suitably attired for a walk in the woods, she set out onto the trail, grabbing one of the paper trail maps stored in a plastic bin at the trail entrance. According to the map, it was only a half mile to the waterfall, and the trail difficulty was rated "Moderate." Since Joanna was a veteran of some of the toughest hiking trails in the eastern Appalachians, this would be just a pleasant evening stroll.

Joanna set out on the trail, knocking her carved walking stick into the soft forest loam with every step. The rhododendrons and mountain azaleas lining the trail were already in full bloom, filling the mountain air with their light, sweet scent. The late afternoon sun's rays bent through the trees into a hundred prisms of light. The sheer beauty of the mountain locale took her breath away.

Before she knew it, Joanna reached Elk Falls. She was stunned by the incredible sight of the falls, which were almost a hundred feet high and gushing with thousands of gallons of mountain water, fresh from the spring runoff. The sound of rushing water was almost deafening, and yet soothing at the same time. The limestone falls were already green with lichens and moss, and the air was heady with the combined scents of mineral water, forest loam, blooming mountain azaleas, and wet rock. Joanna closed her eyes and breathed in this luscious perfume, which released all the remaining sexual tension from her body almost immediately.

Joanna set her walking stick and flashlight aside and settled down onto a flat, dry rock for a rest. Soon she fell into an almost meditative state, lulled into semiconsciousness from the sound of constantly rushing water and the delightful sights and smells of the late evening North Carolina mountains.

After resting, eyes closed in the kind of serene afterglow only a close encounter with nature can provide, Joanna was jolted by the sound of an unfamiliar man's voice.

"You all right, ma'am?"

Joanna jerked awake. To her shock and dismay, she found herself sitting in pitch darkness. She glanced at her glow-in-the-dark Timex watch and saw it was approaching eight thirty. She'd been meditating—perhaps even napping—for over two hours! Mortified at her foolish actions, Joanna turned her head towards the voice, dreading what she might discover.

Joanna's eyes fell upon a portly middle-aged man in coveralls, carrying a Coleman lantern that did little to penetrate the heavy darkness of the forest. He was of medium height and had brownish hair, but Joanna couldn't discern much more than that in the blackness. And she wasn't about to move closer to the man to get a better look—at least, not until she figured out if he was friend or foe.

The man leaned closer, and Joanna could see he had a gentle, friendly face. A face that reminded her of someone, in fact. But she couldn't quite place who. "Ma'am, it's not a good idea to fall asleep alone in these woods," the stranger said.

"I know," Joanna muttered. Experienced hiker that she was, she should have known better than to fall so completely under the spell of a simple waterfall, no matter how beautiful it might be. "I just—I guess I just lost track of the time."

"I'd say so," the older man said. "You're lucky we found you when we did. There's lots of black bear in these woods, and they come out at night to eat. We'll help you get back to your car if you like."

We?

"There are more of you, sir?" Joanna asked, feeling stupid and scared at the same time.

"Yes, Joanna, there are," a familiar voice said from somewhere in the trees. Dr. Harlan Wilkinson stepped out of the shadows to stand next to the portly man holding the lantern. Harlan was in camouflage hunting clothes, and in his uninjured left hand, he carried a lightweight .38 hunting rifle with a scope.

Joanna nearly fainted at the sight of him. "Wh-what? Harlan? What on earth are you doing here?"

"Just doing a spot of hunting," Harlan replied, his voice almost a chuckle. "Joanna, this is my cousin, Richard."

"Richard Wilkinson," the portly man added, setting his lantern on the rock beside her and extending his hand for her to shake. "Pleased to meet you, ma'am. I take it you and my cousin are already acquainted?"

"Ummm, yes." Joanna didn't shake the man's hand, and he folded it back by his side without comment. She was positively reeling. What were the odds that Harlan Wilkinson would appear in the exact remote, complete-middle-of-nowhere spot that she had picked at random for the sole purpose of trying to forget him?

One in a million, at least.

Joanna felt her face go red as a blowtorch. She was embarrassed, nervous, frightened, and awestruck all at once. Was this one-in-a-million shot – the object of her desire finding her in such a bizarre, random way – a cosmic message of some kind? An incredible stroke of luck? A coincidence worthy of the sappiest soap opera?

Or in some crazy, inexplicable way, had she *meant* for this to happen?

Harlan inched closer to her. She could smell his scent – the same mix of aftershave and delightfully male musk that she'd smelled back in Raleigh, only by now the alcohol was worn off. "Joanna, if you were so desperate to run into me tonight, why didn't you just wait around the restaurant for a few minutes longer? I came back looking for you, but you'd already left." Harlan Wilkinson shined his flashlight into his face, shooting her a quizzical look. He seemed as mystified at their chance meeting as she.

Or was he? Perhaps this strange occurrence was just another opportunity for Harlan to drive Joanna mad. For all she knew, he had followed her here.

Whatever had really happened, Joanna decided the best thing to do was to get back to the relative safety of her vehicle as soon as possible. She stood up and headed for the trail, expecting the two men to follow her. They did.

Silently, Harlan and Richard escorted Joanna back to her car, using Richard's lantern and Joanna's and Harlan's flashlights to guide the way. Harlan kept his rifle at the ready, on guard against any possible nighttime predators – bears, coyotes, or who knew what – but it proved unnecessary. Within less than ten minutes, Joanna was back in the small trailhead parking lot, which was brightly lit by a single halogen lamp. As if he understood that there was unfinished business between Harlan and Joanna, Richard walked to the far side of the parking lot until he was out of earshot.

Joanna folded her arms across her chest angrily. "How *dare* you leave me alone in the restaurant like that!" she shouted at him, making no effort to lower her voice. Her shouts echoed off the mountains and trees into scores of reverberations that sounded almost animal-like. "And after the public scene you pulled, too – why did you have to humiliate me?" Joanna was so livid she had to fight back tears. But even so, just being in Harlan's presence again set her heart to hammering.

Harlan's face, crossed by the harsh shadows cast by the halogen lamp, showed no emotion. "I'm sorry, Joanna, but I just had to leave. Your comments – well, they kind of put me in a bad way, and

I didn't want to risk hurting your feelings more than I already had. I needed to go somewhere to cool off for a few minutes. So I left."

This just made Joanna even more furious. "Then I suppose you think I couldn't have cared less that you ditched and humiliated me in a public place after I'd already gone to the trouble of driving you all the way to Raleigh to see Dr. Rosenblum – who, mind you, re-arranged his whole schedule to see you as a personal favor to me. Not to mention the fact I tried to treat you to a nice meal to calm your nerves?"

"Joanna—"

She balled her fists and stamped her foot. "You thought that abandoning me in a public place wouldn't bother me, after all that? Is that what you thought, Harlan Wilkinson? Huh?" Joanna's breath was coming only in gasps. She was unsure if it was because she was so furious – or just wildly aroused.

Harlan raised one eyebrow. "Joanna, I needed to cool down. That's all. You're acting as if I physically abused you or something."

"You might as well have." Joanna was almost hyperventilating. She realized now that being out of Harlan's presence for more than a few hours almost *was* like being physically abused. She needed him – needed his touch, his kiss, his hands on her so badly that being separated from him actually hurt her physically.

Harlan inched closer to her. "Joanna, are you all right?"

"No." Joanna matched his step with two of her own, until their faces were only inches apart, their shoulders and chests touching. Joanna felt her nipples go rock-hard against the fabric of Harlan's rough hunting jacket. She ran one of her hands up and down along his firm, muscular chest, tracing the outline of his pecs through the layers of his hunting attire's ripstop nylon fabric. She heard Harlan's breath catch, felt him leaning into her, felt him plunging his hands into her hair.

"Joanna—" Harlan breathed, and his mouth seized upon hers. They kissed for a long time – so long that Joanna had to break off the kisses several times just to come up for air. They were long, slow, wet kisses, done with both passion and caution. Harlan's tongue eased in and out of Joanna's mouth in a series of tiny, feathery movements, as if he was almost afraid of making full contact with her. In response,

Joanna sought Harlan's mouth and lips with more and more abandon, finally sinking her teeth into the inside of his lower lip with scores of light, bouncing nibbles, each little bite spaced between deep, sweeping probes with her tongue. Harlan groaned, clicked on the safety on his rifle, set it down beside his feet, and slid his hands down Joanna's back to grip her buttocks. With his uninjured left hand, he grabbed fistfuls of her nurse's uniform slacks, then pinched at her firm, rounded flesh hard enough to leave marks. Joanna felt herself go wet as Harlan's crotch hardened into a tight, thick bulge against her thigh. She reached down for it, gently stroking his need through the layers of his clothing. Harlan groaned again, more urgently this time.

God only knew how long they'd been embracing, kissing, exploring each other's bodies when they heard a loud, forced cough from the other end of the parking lot.

Apparently Harlan's cousin Richard wasn't interested in a peep show.

Harlan broke away from her. The space that grew between them cut her like a hundred pointed daggers. "We ahhh, should probably stop this," he said. "At least, for now."

Joanna nodded. Every pore of her body was ringing with spicy-hot sensations, with a need that had to be satisfied – *now*. No matter how much her head – or even her heart – told her that Harlan was bad for her, was unstable and unpredictable, was possibly even dangerous, it just made her want him all the more.

"I'll walk you to your car," Harlan said, forcefully taking her arm and leading her there. Somehow, she managed to get her car keys out of her hip pocket and unlock the door. Harlan helped set her in the Honda's driver's seat, but she was trembling so much she could barely stay upright, let alone drive.

"Would you like me to drive you home?" he asked. "I can hunt with Richard another time."

Joanna nodded, still shaking uncontrollably.

"Pardon me a minute," Harlan said, and picking up his rifle from the spot where he'd left it, he sauntered over to where his cousin was standing. Joanna's cheeks colored at the thought of the amorous sight she and Harlan had just provided him.

A moment later, Harlan returned to the Honda. He'd left his rifle with Richard, from whom he must have borrowed it. He carried a small backpack that Joanna assumed must hold his street clothes. Instead of having her get out of the car, Harlan simply lifted her up and moved her over to the passenger seat, then took his place behind the wheel. Gently, he forced her keys from her clenched fist and started the ignition.

"I think we should head back to Statesville before continuing...what we just started. I've sobered up, and my hand is stitched up well enough that I should be able to manage driving. Is that all right with you, Joanna?"

Joanna nodded again, then leaned forward to rest her forehead on the dashboard. She suddenly felt very faint.

"Are you sure you're all right?" He reached over to caress her hair softly. This soothed her a little. But even this gentle, ministering touch burned her in places that wouldn't be still for long. She wasn't sure how much more she could stand. She needed Harlan back inside her *now*.

After a deep breath, Joanna set herself upright and pulled the seatbelt around her still-heaving body. "I'll be all right. Just take me to my condo, please. I live on Sander Drive, which is just two blocks off Main Street."

Harlan eased the car onto the gravel road that led back to the main highway. "It's still almost an hour and a half drive to Statesville. Can you wait that long? I don't want to rush you or anything, but you seem – very, ahhhh–" Harlan's voice trailed off. Joanna glanced over at him and could tell that he was smirking a little. "Maybe we could find a motel somewhere close by? I think there are a couple in the next town."

Joanna cut him off. "Harlan, I just want you to know that I don't go throwing myself at every man that comes into my life."

"I never said you did."

"I am usually very reserved when it comes to – interpersonal relations," Joanna said, feeling ridiculous.

"I'm sure you are," Harlan replied. Now it was obvious he was trying hard not to laugh.

"Don't make fun of me!" Joanna hissed, offended. "It's just that—it's just that-"

"What?" The car made it to the main road and Harlan glanced in both directions before pulling the car onto the deserted, dark highway. He drove with his left hand, keeping his injured right one in his lap. Joanna silently thanked God her Honda had an automatic transmission.

"It's just that nobody has made me feel this way before." There. She had said it. Dr. Harlan Wilkinson had awakened the sensual, sexual woman she had buried deep inside herself for her entire life. And then some. He had uncovered some unknown part of her that she hadn't known she possessed. A part of her that was capable of desires and sensations she'd never experienced before, that she'd never even thought possible. Her body ached for Harlan's touch. Her mouth yearned for his lips on hers, for the gentle probing of his tongue. Her body's private depths burned for the fulfillment only prolonged, ardent lovemaking with Harlan could provide.

And the thought of each and every one of the ninety minutes that made up the long drive to Statesville and separating her from that fulfillment was pure torture.

Joanna grabbed Harlan's hand on the steering wheel. "Stop the car," she ordered.

"What?" Harlan struggled to keep his eyes on the road. "Why?"

"I want – I *need* – you to take me right now, Harlan. Please."

Harlan gently loosened Joanna's hand from the wheel and set it in her lap, all the time keeping the car in motion by steering with his knees. "Are you sure you're ready?"

"I *know* I'm ready, Harlan. Now."

"All right," he said. "It's about three miles to the next exit—"

Joanna pounded her fist against the dashboard. She couldn't wait three miles. "*Now*," she ordered.

Harlan chuckled. "You're the boss," he said. He scanned the roadway for a place to pull over, and saw a wide shoulder alongside the road just ahead. The spot was sheltered by a large hill that formed a high cliff since it had been blasted through to build the highway. There was a small cove indentation in the side of the blasted-out bedrock that would protect them from traffic and onlookers. "I think that'll do nicely." Harlan pulled off the road, tucked the Honda into the little cove, and switched off the headlights. Now they were in total darkness, the only illumination coming from the occasional passing car.

"Well, Joanna?" Harlan said through the darkness. "How do you want to do this? Your wish is my command."

Joanna smiled. She liked the idea of being in charge. God knew she'd never called the shots in her sex life with Bob, and turning the tables on a man as confident and powerful as Harlan was even more enticing. "Get in the backseat," she ordered.

Harlan obeyed. He got out of the car and opened the rear passenger door. He seated himself behind Joanna and smiled, his white, even teeth glowing in the darkness. "Well, I'm here," he said. "What do you want me to do now?"

Joanna giggled. "Take your pants off," she said. "And get a condom on. I'll be right there."

And she was. Joanna jumped into the back of the car, giddy as a teenager on prom night. An unseen force had taken over her body, propelling her head-on into the wild world of roadside sex. Her nurse's top and scrub bottoms were off before her behind could meet the worn upholstery of the Honda's backseat. Her bra was next. She flung it across the car, it landed on the rearview mirror. She saved the panties for last. They ended up impaled on the gearshift, an obvious metaphor for what was about to happen.

There she was, naked in the pitch blackness. A passing car's headlights illuminated her full, round, white breasts, the beams highlighting her erect red nipples. Harlan's breathing got labored as he took in the beautiful sight.

Joanna reached out through the darkness until her hand landed on Harlan's manhood. His pants were unbuttoned, but still on, and the nuclear warhead was back in his pocket, just waiting to launch and explode. All she had to do was push the button.

And push the button she did.

The same unseen force that had stripped Joanna naked on the side of a public highway managed to get Harlan naked in a hurry, too. His shoes and socks ended up on the rear dashboard, his pants on the floor draped over the drive-train hump. His shirt he unbuttoned but kept on, something that Joanna found wildly sexy. She traced the outline of his pecs with one finger on her right hand, and used her left to adjust his equipment to the exact angle she wanted. He leaned forward to kiss her, but Joanna had other plans. Before he could say boo, Joanna was impaled on him.

She rode him like a rodeo bull, hanging on for dear life while he rocked and rolled her, meeting every one of her wild cowgirl moves with one of his own. They continued on this way in the Honda's backseat like a couple of hormone-crazed high-school kids. Until the heat from their bodies steamed up the windows and filled inside of the car until it became a sauna.

Harlan touched her most intimate spot, and set her on fire. Finally the floodgates burst, sending Joanna's whole body into spasms so intense she thought she might split in two.

Harlan finally exploded into her when she thought she couldn't take another second of the mind-numbing pleasure. He collapsed onto her back and sighed. "That was fantastic, Joanna." He whispered. "You are one hell of a hot lay."

She felt herself blush. "Nobody's every called me a hot lay before."

He pulled out and sat up beside her, patted her gently on the buttocks. "I find that very hard to believe."

Joanna sat up and folded her arms across her bare breasts, suddenly shy. "I actually never had much of a sex life before now," she admitted, feeling her cheeks go even redder.

Harlan reached over to stroke her cheek. "Well, that's a travesty," he said. After a long moment, he said "You haven't told me much about yourself, Joanna."

"There's not much to tell," she replied, nervously chewing on a hangnail.

"Tell it anyway." Harlan stroked her cheek again before returning his bandaged right hand to his lap.

"Well, I'm divorced," Joanna said, uneasy about revealing too much about herself too soon. There was so much about her marriage to Bob that was still painful to her. "My parents are both dead, and I was an only child, so I don't have any close relatives living. I grew up in Statesville and went to the University of North Carolina for nursing school. I've lived in North Carolina for almost all my life, except for the three years I spent as an Army nurse."

"You mentioned you had spent some time in the military," Harlan said. "That's interesting. *Very* interesting." Even in the dim moonlight, Joanna could see that Harlan was smirking again.

"Why?"

Harlan wrapped his arm around Joanna's bare shoulders and pulled her tenderly against his body. "You just don't seem like the Army type, is all."

"That's because I'm not," Joanna replied. "The only reason I joined the Army was to help pay off my school loans. And to travel."

"I see." Harlan cleared his throat. "So, I take it the only traveling you've done was during your time in the Army?"

"Yes," Joanna said, her voice clipped. "Except for my honeymoon in Las Vegas, but that was only for three days."

"Why haven't you traveled more on your own, Joanna?" Harlan asked. "You seem to be someone who would enjoy it, especially given how much you seem to know about food and wine."

This touched a raw nerve with Joanna. She hadn't grown up in a life of privilege or extravagance, as she suspected Harlan probably had. Although they had raised her with the ladylike manners and traditional values of a Southern belle, Joanna's parents were poor North Carolina mill workers who had died young and left her no inheritance but their many unpaid debts. College had been a luxury she'd scrimped, saved, and served three hardship-filled years in the Army to pay for. Her ex-husband Bob had had a good income, but he'd also been a spendthrift during their marriage, leaving her worse off financially after her marriage than before. And Joanna hardly considered herself cultured—what little she knew about foreign cuisines and wines she'd learned from library books.

"This may be news to you, Harlan, but there are people in this world who can't just pick up and go to the other side of the world at the drop of a hat," Joanna replied, curtly. "I've never had much money. I've always had to work for a living."

Harlan did not say anything for several minutes. He pulled away from her and leaned against the car door. Joanna glanced over at him and saw the familiar pattern of nervous tics rippling along his jaw.

After what seemed like an eternity, Harlan finally responded. "Joanna, I assume that remark is supposed to imply that I am some kind of spoiled brat from a rich and powerful family, that I've just had everything handed to me on a silver platter or something. I am here to tell you that nothing could be further from the truth. In fact, Joanna, you and I have pretty similar backgrounds."

"I have a hard time believing that," Joanna chirped, although she *had* found the fact that Harlan had a middle-aged cousin who spoke and acted just like a native North Carolinian a bit odd.

"Well, it's true." Harlan hunched up his neck and shoulders, obviously tense. "I might be a wealthy and successful surgeon now —and maybe not for long if my hand doesn't heal properly – but I wasn't always wealthy or successful. Not by a long shot."

"Hmm," was the only response Joanna could manage.

"My parents died in a car accident when I was still a freshman in college. My father was a university professor at the small private college that I was attending just outside of Boston, so I got free tuition my first year. But after that I was on my own. My mother was a housewife, and my dad's college-professor salary was never good. He was from a pretty poor family himself – in fact, he was originally from Asheville, North Carolina, just a few hours away from here. I still have relatives in North Carolina. Like my cousin Richard, who you just met."

"Hmm," Joanna grunted again. She was fast growing embarrassed at the way she'd pre-judged Harlan as being just another wealthy, arrogant Yankee – when in fact he was only a generation removed from the same kind of rural mountain upbringing as her own.

Harlan seemed to notice her embarrassment. His tone of voice softened a bit. "Like I said, my family wasn't well off. They died when I was only nineteen, and my brothers and sisters were all still just kids. Mom and Dad didn't leave us much in the will, and what they did leave got divided up among four siblings. So I pretty much had to work my way through college, and then medical school and residency at UMass, getting by mostly on loans – which were gargantuan by the time I finally finished my residency training. So I, like you, joined the Army to help pay them off. I was an Army surgeon for eight years. I served in Desert Storm too, just like you did. I was mostly stationed in Turkey, but I did spend some time at Walter Reed in the early '90s. I'm surprised the two of us never ran into each other there. Maybe we were there at different times and just missed each other."

Joanna was stunned. Harlan's life story was sounding more and more like her own. Flushing red, all she could do was look down at the dirty floorboards of her car.

"I got out of the Army just after Desert Storm," Harlan went on. "I'd had the opportunity to get some important research articles on surgical infections and other topics published as a direct result of my Army work, and that led me to get several lucrative faculty offers from research hospitals. I finally settled on Hofts. After I'd been at Hofts for a couple of years, one of my colleagues urged me to accompany her on a trip to Africa with Doctors Without Borders to help treat victims of Sudan's civil war. I jumped at the offer. I took an unpaid sabbatical from Hofts and went to the Sudan for eight months."

"What was that like?" Joanna asked, genuinely curious. She'd always dreamed of volunteering her nursing skills overseas, but she'd never been able to afford to take the time off from her regular job.

Harlan sighed audibly. "Well, at first it was absolutely terrible. The things I saw there – horrible, unbelievable things – they just defy description."

Harlan said nothing more for several minutes. Joanna didn't press him; she could tell that every word in his Sudan story came with great difficulty. She leaned back in her seat, waiting for Harlan to tell the rest of his tale in his own time.

After several minutes, Harlan pulled Joanna closer and began to stroke her hair. "It took me a month or two to adjust to that horrific environment. There are literally stretches of days and weeks during my first few months in the Sudan that I have completely blacked out. But once I was there a while, I found that the medicine I was practicing among the refugees and tribesmen was doing a lot of good. I saw with my own eyes that even in the midst of all that wretchedness and human misery, one person – one surgeon – could do a hell of a lot of good. And I was fortunate to be working with a lot of very, very good people, who collectively did a *huge* amount of good. Joanna, my time in Doctors Without Borders was the first thing I ever experienced that made me completely proud of the fact that I am a physician."

This surprised Joanna. "You mean you weren't proud of that before?"

Harlan sighed again. "Joanna, to be quite honest, I originally became a doctor principally to make money. I didn't exactly grow up poor, but in a family with four kids living on a college professor's salary we weren't exactly well-to-do, either. Then when my parents died and I was on my own – I knew that in order to continue my education, I would have to take out loans – and then I would have to find some kind of job that would allow me to pay the loans back and still have enough money left over to live some kind of comfortable life. The Army helped with some of the bills, but not all of them. I saw medicine as a means to make a comfortable living, and I also found that I was good at it. Sure, I took the Hippocratic Oath, swore to "do no harm" and all that, but until I went to the Sudan, I was in the profession for the money, not necessarily to help serve humanity."

"If that's really how you felt, then why did you go to the Sudan in the first place? You could have made more money by staying home."

Harlan laughed. "Well, that's kind of a funny story."

"So tell it."

"The colleague who urged me to go with her to the Sudan was the woman who eventually became my wife. I agreed to go because I had a crush on her. I figured that spending time with her in a remote, dangerous place would help me seduce her more easily. And that's exactly what happened."

Joanna's eyes flew wide. Still, given what had just transpired between to two of them, she wasn't exactly surprised. "You went all the way to the Sudan just so you could have sex with a woman?"

"Precisely."

"So, where is this woman now?" Joanna asked. She'd noticed days ago that Harlan wore no wedding ring.

Harlan stiffened. "She's dead."

"I see," Joanna said in a small voice. "What happened to her?"

"I don't want to talk about it."

"But—"

Harlan pulled away. "I already said I don't want to discuss it."

"I'm sorry," Joanna said in a small voice.

Harlan did not answer. Instead he gathered up his clothes from the car's floorboards and got dressed. "We should probably get going," he said. "We don't want to risk getting picked up half-naked by the highway patrol."

Suddenly, Joanna understood the deep look of pain she'd detected in Harlan's eyes from their first meeting. She understood now why a part of him always deemed dangerous just below the surface – even why he'd earned the nickname "Darth Vader" among the Covington Hospital nurses. He'd lost the woman he loved—probably violently. Joanna guessed that his wife must have died on one of their Doctors Without Borders trips, perhaps in the Sudan, perhaps somewhere else.

But where? And how?

As she got dressed, a hundred possible scenarios ran through Joanna's mind. Had Harlan's wife died in a war's crossfire, or perhaps from stepping on a land mine? Had she died of a horrible tropical disease? Kidnapped by bandits? Or worse? Joanna shuddered. She couldn't think of anything worse than having someone you love die young and violently in a foreign land. But it had to be true. There was no other explanation for Harlan's dark side – not as far as she could tell, anyway.

Joanna decided not to broach the subject with him again. She would show him patience, kindness, and understanding – not to mention physical passion. And then, once he trusted her completely, perhaps Harlan could share his demons with her, maybe even come to terms with them.

Chapter Fifteen

AFTER ANOTHER hour or so of highway driving, Joanna and Harlan were approaching the outskirts of Statesville. They'd be home in a few minutes, and Joanna's body buzzed at the prospect of persuading Harlan to join her in her queen-sized bed. After their conversation turned sour following their roadside tryst, Joanna wasn't sure she'd get the privilege of bedding Harlan again anytime soon. But she could still test the waters. She gently placed her hand on Harlan's knee as he drove. He didn't look down or acknowledge her gesture in any way, but he didn't rebuff her, either. A good sign.

As Harlan pulled the car off the freeway and onto the Statesville exit ramp the anticipation building in her nether parts as she counted down the landmarks between the freeway and her home was too much for her to bear. She needed a quick fix, and she couldn't wait even the five minutes it would take to drive home and get inside her condo.

"Harlan, pull over, please."

He glanced at her sideways. "But we're almost to your house."

"Pull over."

Harlan looked for a suitable spot, and selected the empty parking lot of a doughnut shop that had closed for the evening. The doughnut shop was only two blocks from her condo, but Joanna's need for some more sensual satisfaction was too urgent even to wait that long. Harlan parked the car and switched off the engine. "Now Joanna, I really think it won't hurt if we wait just a few minutes more—"

She cut him off by way of unbuttoning his fly. It was obvious he was as ready to go as she was. "At least let me give you a sneak preview," she cooed.

She closed her mouth around him. At first Harlan writhed in shock at the sudden wetness of her mouth on his most sensitive organ, but he soon settled right into it. "Mmmmmmmm," he groaned, relishing every move Joanna's mouth and tongue made. "This is so, so good, Joanna. But I think I know how to make it even better."

Joanna looked up and pulled away. "What exactly did you have in mind?"

"Watch," he replied. Then he keyed the ignition. "Go back to what you were doing, Joanna."

She stared back at him, wide-eyed. "You want me to do this while you drive?"

He nodded.

She went down on him as soon as his foot hit the gas.

Joanna was thankful that it was dark and the streets deserted, because any passing driver or pedestrian could have seen the unladylike obscenity happening right in her own vehicle. Harlan's breathing became more and more labored as he drove into her condo building's well-lit parking lot. He slid the car into a parking space directly opposite Joanna's front door, and settled back into the front seat while Joanna brought him to climax.

Joanna had never done anything like this before. A whole new world of sensual freedom had just opened itself up to her.

But it seemed that new world wasn't going to last very long.

The moment was interrupted by a loud banging against the car's roof. Joanna looked up from Harlan's lap and out the driver's side window. She was shocked by what she saw there.

Joanna's ex-husband Bob was standing in front of the car, pounding his fists against the Honda's rusty roof. He'd obviously watched the whole thing.

And Bob did not look happy.

Chapter Sixteen

HARLAN BARELY had enough time to stuff himself back into his pants before Bob started trying to break into the Honda. Joanna leaped out of the car and put herself between it and her ex-husband, who had picked up a tree branch from the side of the parking lot and looked about two seconds away from ramming it through the windshield. Joanna remembered a snippet of her Army self-defense training and managed to get the thing out of his hands before any damage was done. But Harlan was right behind her, ready to throw a punch with his good hand if need be.

"Bob!" Joanna shouted once she'd gotten control of the situation. "What in God's name are you doing here?"

"Well, I'm not here to get jerked off," he hissed. "Unlike your lucky friend here."

This didn't sit well with Harlan. He rolled up his sleeves and looked seconds away from sucker-punching Bob. "Now see here—"

Joanna held up her hand, calling him off. "It's all right, Harlan. I can handle this just fine on my own. Stand back and give us some room, please." He obeyed, but was none too happy about it.

Bob had always had a lousy sense of timing, and today was no exception. "I've been trying to reach you all day," he snapped, taking no notice of Harlan and thrusting himself right into Joanna's face. "I called you at the hospital, and they said you weren't there.

I called you at home, and you weren't there. I called your cell, but got a recording that the number was out of service."

Joanna had changed her cell phone number three weeks earlier solely to keep Bob from bothering her. "Bob, please leave. I don't want you here." Joanna tried to walk past him to her front door, but Bob blocked her path.

"I won't leave," Bob shot back, grabbing Joanna by the shoulder. "You and I have some unfinished business to take care of."

"No, we don't," Joanna hissed, wrestling away from him. "Bob, we're divorced. Our marriage is over. Accept it. I have." And to illustrate her point, she grabbed Harlan's arm and pulled him close to her.

"I'm not here to try to win you back, Joanna," Bob retorted. "But I am here to talk to you about our finances—"

"*Your* finances," Joanna quipped. She could already tell where this was going. "When we got divorced, your money problems became yours alone. Remember? The judge even said so himself."

Undeterred, Bob clenched his fists and inched in closer. "Joanna, I came here to ask you for a loan. And after what you put me through in our marriage, you owe me."

At this, Joanna actually laughed. "Ha! Get real, Bob. Our marriage was a total joke and you know it. We didn't even have sex for the last two years we were living under the same roof, for God's sake. And I'm up to my eyeballs in debt because of you as it is. I'll be paying off my share of the marital debt for the next six years. Or have you forgotten? And now you actually have the balls to show up here and ask me for *more* money?"

Bob's face fell. "Joanna, this isn't like all the other times. This is different."

Joanna scoffed. "Bob, even if I *did* want to loan you more money – which I don't – I don't have anything left to give. I'm flat broke. Between your out-of-control spending habits and your desire to invest in every pyramid scheme ever invented, I'm lucky I still have a roof over my head."

Bob flinched at this, but then strengthened his resolve. He glanced from Joanna to Harlan, and back to Joanna again. "Joanna, that's not true. I happen to know that as long as you're bonking Dr. Money-bags here, you have access to as much cash as you want. How much is he paying you to mess around with him like that, anyway?"

Joanna's jaw dropped. "Excuse me?"

Harlan clenched his uninjured fist. "I'm warning you, buddy—"

Bob didn't back down. "No, I'm warning *you*," he yelled, wagging his finger in Harlan's face. "I know a lot about you already, Dr. Wilkinson. Yeah, that's right, I know your name. My attorney's been looking into your background, and it seems to me you and my ex-wife are into some kind of sleazy business together. And I don't mean between the sheets, either."

Harlan clenched his teeth. "I'm afraid I don't know what you mean."

Bob grinned. "Don't give me that crap. I know all about what happened to you back in Boston. And I know what kind of financial arrangements you have set up with Covington Community Hospital, too. Looks to me you're hot-'n-heavy with my ex-wife here just so you can create a distraction for what's really going on over at the hospital."

Joanna gasped. She glanced from her heaving ex-husband to an increasingly red-faced and nervous Harlan, and back again. It was obvious that her ex had touched a nerve with him – and a deep one at that. What did Bob know that she didn't?

"I'd watch your back if I were you, Doctor," Bob went on. "My ex-wife is a cold, conniving bitch who's probably only interested in your money. God knows she needs some. And so do I. Joanna, my attorney will be in touch."

"I don't know what for, Bob," she sputtered. "We're divorced. We don't have anything to do with each other anymore."

"Not if I can help it," he shot back. "My attorney will explain everything to you tomorrow."

With that, Bob turned on his heel, got into his battered Geo Metro, and drove away.

As soon as Bob was out of sight, Joanna spun around and faced Harlan, who by now had gone almost purple with rage. "What was Bob insinuating, Harlan?" she demanded. "He obviously knows something about you. And I know Bob well enough to know that he understands how to sniff out money – especially *dirty* money. He's made a whole career out of trying to rip people off."

Harlan didn't answer. He just huffed and puffed and kicked at the dust on the asphalt.

That didn't sit well with Joanna. "Harlan, I know we're not exactly the romance of the century right now. I can accept that. But if you're really using me to cover up something unsavory at work, I think I'm entitled to know. My career is on the line, after all."

Harlan took a deep breath and blew it out. "I'm not using you, Joanna. Please trust me when I tell you that what your husband is insinuating is totally false."

"*Ex*-husband," she corrected. "If that's so, why does your head look like it's about to explode?"

Harland didn't answer. He just stared at the ground.

Joanna felt her stomach drop. "Harlan, if you can't be honest with me about this, I think it's time you went home."

He gave her a single nod. "I'll call myself a cab," he said.

That's it? Joanna thought. *He's not even going to argue?*

That probably meant Bob was telling the truth.

Joanna's heart sank as she watched Harlan walk away from her and go stand on the corner. He called a cab with his cell phone, and five minutes later, he was gone.

Chapter Seventeen

SHIRLEY HAD had her fun with Dr. Grenoway. Now it was time to move on to the next big thing.

The only question was, where would the next best thing come from? The pickings around town were pretty slim, after all. Dr. Grenoway was the only hot-to-trot young male surgical resident in the whole hospital. And now she'd already been there, done that. But there had to be at least a few attractive, eligible young men floating around the hospital. The only question was, where?

It was high time for her to start expanding her horizons beyond the operating room.

As she stood under the locker room showerhead, scrubbing off the remnants of both a long day's work in the OR and the scent of Dr. Grenoway, Shirley silently wondered to herself, *If I were a hot young single guy under the age of twenty-five with a hospital job and I weren't a doctor, where would I work?*

The answer came to her in a split second.

The Janitorial department. That's where the orderlies worked— young men, all of them. And pretty much all the orderlies were cute, fit, and under twenty-five. Hell, a few of them were under *twenty-one* – fresh meat right out of high school. Shirley knew that the bright young things who pushed gurneys and swept up vomit for eight bucks an hour would be easy pickings. Some of them were probably virgins, too – looking for their first sensual experiences, preferably with a sophisticated older woman like herself. Shirley licked her lips at the thought of just how luscious those kinds of encounters could be. If things went her way, those trysts would make her wild evening with Jason The Drunken Frat boy look like child's play.

And if Shirley's escapades among the orderlies went well, she'd move right on up to the cafeteria, where she knew local college students worked part time. And then maybe she could check out some X-ray technicians. There were a bunch of those over in Radiology, not a one of them over the age of thirty.

The possibilities for sex in this small community hospital alone were endless – if only one knew where to look.

Why didn't she think of this before?

Maybe it was because she was a repressed, stressed-out ball of nerves before. It was really amazing what a few good rolls in the hay could do for the psyche – Shirley was seeing opportunities right under her nose that she'd never known existed. And she had Dr. Harlan Wilkinson to thank for it. Unbeknownst to him, he'd inspired her to open up and explore her long-hidden sensual self.

Shirley rinsed off and stepped out of the shower. As she wrapped a towel around herself, she knew what the final step in her newfound adventures would be.

Once she'd had her way with the hot young boy-toys scattered around the hospital, she'd shift her attentions to conquering the man who'd inspired her sexual transformation in the first place. Sure, the man was obnoxious as hell – a cool and charismatic McDreamy he sure wasn't – but he was still smoking hot. And if the beautiful and sensual Joanna Watson could get into his pants (as Shirley now knew she had—the tender way she'd reacted to his palm-slicing made that pretty obvious), why couldn't Shirley? She'd already managed to seduce a boy-toy almost half her age *and* a handsome, *engaged* doctor-in-training in less than two days' time.

Shirley knew now that she obviously had what it took to get any man she wanted. And that knowledge was powerful, indeed. Because now Shirley also knew that she had the power to take back what Joanna Watson had stolen from her.

And she would stop at nothing to make that happen.

Chapter Eighteen

AS JOANNA watched Harlan walk away from her and disappear into his cab, she felt sick to her stomach. He'd just rejected her – and in the worst way possible. Joanna had never taken rejection well —probably why she'd agreed to marry her loser ex-husband Bob in the first place – but this was different. Harlan Wilkinson had refused to look her in the eye and tell her the truth about something she had the feeling was very, very sinister indeed. And in doing so, Harlan had pretty much confirmed Bob's accusations.

Just a few short moments ago Joanna had gone down on Harlan in public, her body so hot with sexual energy that she could barely contain herself in his presence. And now, she stood alone and cold in a parking lot. And all because her ex-husband had shown up out of the blue and pulled the proverbial rose-colored glasses right off her face.

Talk about a twist of fate.

Her heart sinking, Joanna skulked off to her condo. She broke down into sobs as soon as she crossed the threshold. And not just because she now felt dirty and cheap – but because now she knew there would probably never be a chance for her to win Harlan Wilkinson's heart.

Humiliated, she holed herself up in her condo and didn't eat, shower, or speak to anyone for three days.

*****

Even if Joanna Watson was hiding from the world, the world didn't stop turning just because she was holed up in her condo crying her eyes out, guzzling too much cheap vodka from her freezer, and generally feeling sorry for herself.

Her answering machine was loaded with phone messages, all of them unanswered. There were at least twelve angry and frantic ones from her ex-husband Bob, all of which Joanna deleted on the third day. Three or four more from Bob's slimy attorney, who greeted her politely, then ordered her to call him back immediately – or else. Finally, there were at least half a dozen from Maryam Malone at Covington Community Hospital – each one sounding increasingly desperate and nervous.

By the time her vodka had run out on the afternoon of the third day, a half-drunk Joanna finally had the courage to call Maryam at the hospital.

"Surgery and Recovery, this is Maryam," the old nurse answered in her friendly, raspy voice.

"Maryam, it's Joanna."

"Joanna! Why the hell didn't you call me back sooner? I've been trying to reach you for three days."

"Sorry, Maryam," she slurred, smelling the acrid alcohol on her own breath and wincing. "I've been – indisposed."

"Well, Joanna, I just called to tell you that Administration came back with the report on Dr. Wilkinson's surgery accident. It's exactly like you said. They're saying it's his own fault, and he's been placed on paid leave until further notice."

Joanna said nothing. It was just how she'd expected things would go, but the thought of Harlan being disciplined by the hospital administration hurt her terribly. How ironic it was that on the first day she'd known him, Harlan had threatened *her* with administrative discipline. It was an almost karmic coincidence, in fact – yet another painful reminder of the now-severed connection between them. Joanna blinked back tears.

"Joanna, are you all right?" Maryam asked.

"I'm fine, Maryam, really," she lied. "Was there some other reason you were calling?"

"Yes, actually, there was." The older nurse sounded worried. "With Dr. Wilkinson on suspension, we're without an attending surgeon. We've only got senior surgery residents to work with, and they can't get us a temporary attending until at least late next week, maybe longer. So Joe Middleton himself has asked that *you* come back to work right away and help the residents out in the OR. They need someone with a lot of experience to guide them, and you're the closest thing we've got to an attending surgeon until the fill-in guy gets here. I'm afraid you'll have to go back to double and triple shifts for a while, starting today."

Joanna flopped down on her sofa. "But what about my two weeks' vacation? Am I *ever* going to get to take it?"

"I'm afraid not, hon. I'm sorry. I'll try to be as easy on you as I can—just please, *pretty* please, don't quit on me, okay? I'm already short on nurses as it is. And the ones I've still got are acting mighty strange. Like Shirley Daniels. I don't know what's gotten into that woman lately, but her mind's on something other than her job, if you know what I mean."

I know exactly what you mean, Joanna thought to herself. If Maryam only knew what was really going on in the elevators and parking garages of the hospital – the poor old woman would probably drop dead of a heart attack.

"I won't quit Maryam, don't worry," she said, but she knew it was a promise she might not be able to keep.

"When can you come in?" Maryam asked, obviously anxious. "There are two complicated procedures scheduled for this evening, and the residents are nervous about them."

Joanna glanced at her watch. Two o'clock. She'd need at least two hours for the effects of all the cheap booze to wear off, plus another thirty minutes to make herself presentable. "I'll be there at five," she replied.

"Good," Maryam said with a sigh of relief. "Oh, and Joanna, I should warn you. Darth Vader will be back for some of his things sometime this evening. So you might run into him around the department. Word around the hospital is he's very upset with you. Did you do something to piss him off?"

Joanna could think of at least twenty reasons why Harlan might be mad at her, but she wasn't about to discuss them with Maryam, world-class gossiper that she was. "I have no idea," she fibbed. "I'm sure he's just upset about getting placed on leave."

"You're probably right. See you at five. And Joanna, try to take a nap or something before you come in. You sound. . .tired."

Drunk is more like it, Joanna thought. She hung up on Maryam without even saying goodbye.

Chapter Nineteen

SHIRLEY HAD only been doing her latest push for all things hot and sexy for three days, but she was already more successful at it than she'd ever imagined.

She was relaxing in a hot bath at home, taking a brief respite before she had to be back at the hospital at five p.m. to assist on a couple of complicated surgeries. As she sank back into the piles of hot, gardenia-scented suds, her mind wandered back through all the luscious, sexy moments that she'd managed to snag over the past three days and nights.

Mentally revisiting all the naughty behavior she'd engaged in over the past seventy-two hours would be more stimulating than any sexual fantasy she could possibly concoct on her own. Her heartbeat quickened and her body temperature rose as the memories of all her hot, impromptu seductions came flooding back. . . .

*****

She'd been wandering deep in the bowels of the decaying old hospital building Tuesday night when she found her next boy-toy to play with. Shirley had just finished showering upstairs, fresh from her wild stand-up tryst with Dr. Grenoway when she stumbled across the young man who would become her next conquest on her way to drop off an empty ether container.

Sometimes the best scenery was where you least expected it.

After browsing up and down the main corridor, Shirley spied several young men at work—one soldering an electrical panel, another spackling some crumbling plaster, yet another mopping a floor. They were all young and spry, but nothing to write home about. She continued on down the hall into the darker recesses where the toxic material containers were stored, and just when she was about to give up her search for the next big thing, she ran across a gem.

Shirley first saw the gorgeous young man tinkering with a rusty old vertical steam pipe out of the corner of her eye while she dragged the empty pressure-cylinder behind her on a metal dolly. She passed him and walked to the end of the long hallway, where she dropped off the empty ether container with the toothless old sanitary worker responsible for disposing of them properly. Her body already melting with anticipation, Shirley then hustled back down the long corridor and into the abandoned supply room where the beautiful young man was working, blowtorch in hand, safety goggles that did little to hide his deep-set brown eyes and stunning features protecting his face from the flying sparks. Shirley sauntered up to him, taking care to keep a safe distance.

"So, whatchya working on?" she asked, trying to sound casual, even a little masculine. "Doing some welding? That's a very nice-looking blowtorch you've got there." She'd read somewhere—*Cosmopolitan*, probably – that a surefire way to get into a man's pants was to show an interest in tools and heavy machinery.

The young man didn't acknowledge Shirley at first, instead continuing to concentrate on his welding work. He finished that, shut off his blowtorch and set it aside, then picked up a wrench and began adjusting pipe valves – loosening this one, tightening that one. Shirley watched, fascinated. There was a slow, sensual quality to his movements that she found absolutely irresistible. The man couldn't have been more than twenty-five, but he moved with the grace and finesse of a much older, more sophisticated soul. "You're pretty good with that wrench, too," she said.

The gorgeous young welder finally finished his task and turned to face Shirley. He slowly lifted his safety goggles from his chiseled face, and his deep-set brown-black eyes shot her a look so hot it could melt steel. He stood up to his full height – six-foot-two if he was an inch – and flashed her a smile. "Seems to me you're a lady who appreciates a good set of tools," he said.

You have no idea, she thought to herself, feeling her entire lower half burst into flames.

"Can't say as I've ever seen you round these parts," the man said. Shirley detected a hint of a backwoods accent, and for some crazy reason it made her the pit of her stomach flip.

"I'm usually up in the OR," she explained, suddenly feeling a little shy. "I'm a nurse-anesthetist. I wouldn't have been down here at all except I had to bring down an empty ether tank. And we use ether so seldom these days that I've only had two empty canisters my whole career, including this one."

"Well, I guess today is my lucky day, then," he said, grinning even wider. He extended his hand. "My name's George. George Tucker. I'm just about finished up with my work for the day. You off work anytime soon?"

"I'm off now, as a matter of fact," she replied saucily. "I was planning to head out to the parking garage as soon as I dropped off the ether can. But now—"

George cocked an eyebrow. "Let me guess," he said. "Now you've got other plans?"

Shirley fluttered her eyelashes at him. If the look on his face meant what she thought it did, this seduction would be a very easy one. "You could say that," she replied, giving him a slight sashay of the hips, hoping he'd catch her sensual unspoken message.

He did, in spades. "You know, there are an awful lot of cool places to hide down here," he said. "Want me to show you one?"

Shirley nodded.

George packed up his tools into the leather holster belted around his waist and motioned for Shirley to follow him. "Don't you have to punch out first?" she asked.

George shrugged. "Naw, I'm a hired contractor. I just send the hospital a bill for my time every month, then they cut me a check. Nice work if you can get it, I always say. What's your name, miss?"

"Shirley. Shirley Daniels."

"Pleasure to meet you, Shirley. I've always wanted to meet a Shirley. I had a huge crush on Shirley Temple when I was a kid. My grandma had all her movies on video."

She found this hilarious. "Well, now you have. Just don't expect me to break out in a rendition of *Good Ship Lollipop* anytime soon." That got a hearty laugh out of George.

She followed him down a series of twisting, ever-narrower corridors until they ended up in a large, cavern-like room that was full of enormous, condensation-covered steel standpipes and clouds of steam. "This here's the main boiler room," George said. "This building's kind of weird in that both the heating system and the air-conditioning system are both partially steam-powered. It's something out of the 1920s and should have been replaced a million years ago, but what can I say?" He affectionately tapped a pipe. "It keeps me employed. Plus, I've found that this place in particular has a couple nice bonus features, if you catch my drift."

Shirley caught George's drift immediately. "I think we understand each other," she said, dropping her voice a full octave into bedroom territory. "Where do you want to start?"

George cocked his head over towards the darkest corner of the room, where a small nook was carved out of the wall between two large standpipes. "How about over there?"

By way of answering, Shirley sauntered over to the larger of the two standpipes, leaned against it, and dropped her drawers. "Wanna play, George?" she cooed.

He was pressed up against her instantly. "You know it," he said, grinding his groin against her already bare mons. She could feel he was already rock-hard through the thick denim of his work pants. "You don't waste any time, do you, Shirley?"

She pressed back against him with her hips, then reached to unfasten his heavy tool belt. "Well, you know how it is. So many men, so little time. As they say."

George helped her with the tool belt, then went to work getting his cock out of his pants. He pulled a condom out of his wallet and slipped it on. "So you're a girl who gets around, then," he said. "Some guys would have a problem with that, but I don't. I personally think it's pretty cool when a gal isn't afraid to do it with whoever she wants, whenever she wants. Like right now." With that, he opened her seam with one hand, began exploring all her nooks and crannies with the other. He found her epicenter and began to stroke it, up and down, around and around, then penetrated her with two fingers, then three, then *four.* The sensations this man was evoking deep inside her body were positively otherworldly. She was wetter now than she'd ever been in her life.

Shirley came immediately, and with such force she thought her insides would explode.

George didn't miss a beat. As soon as that first orgasm began to subside, he maneuvered his fingers around inside her until he was pressing and caressing her from within, creating an entirely new set of sensations. Shirley came four more times, one right after the other, to the point she thought her entire body would melt into a quivering pile of goo.

And just when she thought she couldn't possibly take any more, George pulled his hand out of her, and in one swift motion flipped her over and took her from behind, pumping her hard and fast. She came one final, earth-shattering time.

Then she blacked out.

*****

When Shirley finally came to, she found herself in an unfamiliar place. She was lying naked in a huge four-poster bed hung with a gauze canopy. The bed was covered in satin sheets and a silk coverlet that was like melted butter against her naked skin, and the room had the musky odor of sex.

How long had she been here? And what – if anything – had happened to her while she was asleep? She had no way of knowing.

Just when she began feeling frightened, a familiar face appeared in the doorway. It was George. "Did you sleep okay?" he asked, snuggling up beside her on the bed. When you blacked out back at the hospital I didn't know what to do, so I brought you here to my house. You've been asleep about five hours. I'm glad you woke up, because if you didn't wake up soon I would have had to call the life squad."

Shirley sat up uneasily. "Did we—ahem—do anything while I was asleep?"

George patted her on the shoulder. "No, babe. I'm too much of a gentleman for that. Though you might wanna wash up a bit."

Shirley blushed, suddenly shy. "Thank you," she whispered.

George stood up and stretched. "The bathroom's just through that door there. And once you're freshened up, I was wondering if you might be interested in a little activity I've got planned for us."

This perked her right up. "Such as?"

George smiled. "Seeing as you're a liberated woman and all, I invited some friends of mine from work over to see if maybe you'd like to get it on with them, too. And me. All of us. Together. What do you think?"

Shirley giggled. "I think I've just died and gone to heaven," she said.

She retired to George's surprisingly luxurious marble bathroom for a shower and a soak in the Jacuzzi. *He must be making some pretty good bucks as a plumbing contractor*, she thought. She languished awhile in the steaming bubbles, her lower body hot and buzzing in anticipation. Today was by far the most exciting day in her mostly uneventful sexual life. What had she done to become such a sexpot so quickly? The answer was confidence.

And that confidence was about to serve her very well. She looked up and saw *three* naked young men standing over her—George of course, and two other young twentysomethings that she vaguely recognized as orderlies at the hospital. All three of these delicious boy-toys had well-developed biceps and washboard abs from all the physical labor they put in on the hospital floor.

And all three of them were hot, throbbing, and ready for action.

Shirley was no longer the repressed, mousy, overworked nobody with no sex life. She was a sex goddess. Now, there was no man she couldn't conquer.

And once she was finished with her crew of boy-toys here, it would be time for her to turn her attentions on Dr. Harlan Wilkinson. She didn't want Harlan out of any personal feelings for him – in fact, she detested the man – she just wanted him on principle. He was the least attainable man in the vicinity, and that made him the most desirable.

Shirley was prepared to do whatever it took to steal him away from Joanna Watson. And if that meant stabbing one of her most respected colleagues in the back – well, so be it.

Chapter Twenty

JOANNA ARRIVED back at Covington Community Hospital a few minutes before five. She headed straight for the Surgery and Recovery locker room to change into fresh sterile scrubs and prepare for the high-risk hysterectomy procedure she was due to assist two senior surgical residents in performing. Normally, a hysterectomy was routine enough for even junior residents to perform alone, but in this case, the procedure was slated for Mrs. Lucinda Small, an eighty-year-old woman with a history of extreme hypertension. Mrs. Small's age and condition raised the possibility for surgical complications tenfold.

Joanna had plenty of experience on high-risk surgeries, which made her well qualified to assist even the most nervous and inexperienced surgery residents. But something about this procedure brought her a sense of dread. Perhaps it was the fact that it would be the first procedure she would assist on without Harlan.

Joanna shook off her unexplained nervousness and headed for the locker room. Shirley Daniels emerged from the showers just as Joanna finished dressing for her shift.

"Fancy seeing you here, Joanna," Shirley said facetiously. "I thought you'd left us for good."

"I was just off for a few days," Joanna retorted. "Administration put me on leave until they could finish their inquiry."

"I don't see why they needed to do an inquiry at all, frankly," Shirley chirped. "It was obvious to everyone that Darth Vader cut his own damn hand."

So Shirley had taken to calling Harlan "Darth Vader" behind his back, too. Joanna wondered if Maryam was responsible for that.

"Darth Vader, huh? Well, it seems you don't think he's Mc-Dreamy anymore," Joanna seethed.

Shirley blinked twice. "I shouldn't have to justify anything to you when it comes to Darth Vader, Joanna. You know firsthand how awful he is to all the nurses. Unless, of course, there's something between the two of you that you aren't telling me."

Joanna gave Shirley a blank stare. She wasn't about to reveal the true goings-on between her and Harlan to anyone at work – least of all Shirley, who was so obviously jealous. Joanna put her personal belongings into her locker and prepared to head out to the post-op ward to get debriefed on the upcoming cases. Before she could get out the locker room door, however, Shirley stopped her.

"Joanna, I don't mean to pry, but is there something going on between you and Darth – I mean, you and Dr. Wilkinson?"

Joanna spun around. She had to work hard not to show any distress in her face at Shirley's question. "What makes you say that?"

"Oh, just a hunch is all." Shirley's smirk was a mile wide.

"I don't know what would give you that idea," Joanna snapped, trying her best to sound indifferent.

Shirley just smiled as she toweled off and got dressed. "See you back in the OR, Joanna. I'll be on anesthesia duty for Mrs. Small's surgery, too. And it looks like we won't have to deal with Darth Vader in there any more, at least. Word on the street is he'll probably have to resign, and good riddance." Then Shirley shot her a look that could cut glass, and said "Then you'll never have to see him again. Won't that be *wonderful*?"

Ouch.

Joanna headed out to the post-op ward, cheeks flaming. All the Recovery beds were empty, but the Intake bin was stuffed with patient files. Apparently there were a number of elective surgeries scheduled for the coming week. Most were routine, but like Mrs.

Small's high-risk hysterectomy scheduled for that evening, along with some complex joint-replacement surgeries, Joanna could see why even the senior residents were worried about the workload. Without an attending surgeon on duty for at least another ten days, Joanna shuddered at the thought of what might happen if Covington's surgery department got saddled with any emergency situations like a serious car accident, severe burns from a house fire, or even bodies mangled by farm equipment. She'd seen all three possibilities happen during her ten years at Covington Community Hospital, and knew any one of these situations could strike at any time, without warning.

She also knew that if any of them happened in the next few days, the hospital would be seriously unprepared. Turning away patients and instead sending them "up the road" to Asheville or Raleigh could result in unnecessary complications, or even fatalities—that much she knew from experience as well. Was stodgy old Joe Middleton's administration really making the right decision by suspending Harlan? Even before his hand injury healed, Harlan could still serve as an expert advisor in the OR to the younger, less-experienced surgeons. He could even do some limited scalpel and suture work with his left hand only, if Joanna assisted. She thought about mentioning this possibility to Administration in an anonymous memo, but ultimately decided against it. In her ten years at the hospital, Joanna had learned the hard way never to interfere with Administration's decisions, no matter how unfair or irrational they might seem.

Joanna was flipping through a double-bypass patient's chart when she heard a familiar masculine voice behind her.

"You didn't waste any time getting back to work, did you?"

Harlan's husky voice hit Joanna's back like a thrown brick. She stiffened at the sound of it, but didn't turn around to acknowledge him.

"I suppose you'll be working here for the rest of your life, won't you, Joanna? A shame, because you're a much better nurse than a cheap community hospital like Covington deserves."

Joanna turned around, slowly. Harlan was looking at her with a mix of anger and indifference. The lines around his eyes seemed deeper somehow, the set of his jaw much sharper and harder than before. The anger marring his face wasn't due to his suspension from duty—it was clear from the look of anguish in his eyes that his fury was much more personal in nature. The incident with Bob at her condo three days before had obviously hurt the man deeply.

"I'm back because Maryam said she needed me," Joanna replied, trying hard to keep her voice even. "The hospital is very short-staffed in Surgery since you got placed on leave. And by the way, Dr. Wilkinson, my future career plans are none of your business."

"Nor mine yours," Harlan seethed. Joanna noticed he was carrying a cardboard box full of office supplies, his many framed diplomas and certificates, and his gold engraved "Harlan J. Wilkinson, MD" nameplate.

"Does that mean you're leaving Statesville?" Joanna asked, nodding at the overloaded box. She was surprised at her own curiosity. She knew she had to keep cool and nonchalant, to give no indication that she still wanted this man desperately. But the sight of Harlan's face and body made that increasingly difficult. She lowered her gaze to the tile floor.

"Again, that's none of your business," Harlan answered curtly. But he didn't leave, either. He stood in the center of the post-op ward, carrying his box of office supplies and medical journals like a lead weight. He looked anxiously back at Joanna, as if he expected her to stop him from leaving somehow. Joanna steeled herself against taking his bait, keeping her eyes down. No matter how much she might want to throw herself into Harlan's arms that very moment, she could not risk the slightest possibility that someone—anyone—would speculate that their relationship was anything more than professional. Especially now that Shirley Daniels was snooping around, following her every move.

"Well, I wish you the best of luck in any case," Joanna finally said. "I don't suppose I'll be seeing you around here much."

"No, I don't suppose you will," Harlan answered.

The sexual tension in the air was so thick you could have cut it with a pair of pinking shears.

Joanna's body cried out its need, its all-consuming desire to fall to her knees and give Harlan a nice good-old-fashioned deep-throat treatment right then and there. But she hardened her heart against the notion with all her might. "Well, I suppose this is goodbye, then," Joanna heard herself say.

"I suppose so." Harlan tightened his grip on the cardboard box and left the room. A lump formed in Joanna's throat as she watched him go. She didn't want to think about the fact it might be the last time she would ever see him.

*****

"Pass me the number four scalpel." Dr. Grenoway – the green surgery resident Shirley had seduced in the locker room—was fumbling his way through Mrs. Small's hysterectomy procedure in the OR two hours later.

"I think you mean the number three, Doctor," she said gently, handing it to him. "The number four is too large for the area you're working on."

"R-Right," the young man mumbled, reaching for the correct scalpel. Then he and Shirley exchanged furtive glances. Joanna wondered why, but she understood soon enough. Despite his surgical mask and plastic faceguard, Joanna could see he was blushing to his hairline. *Those two have been up to something behind closed doors*, she thought.

Dr. Randall Grenoway wasn't exactly the cream of the crop as far as surgical residents were concerned. He'd barely managed to graduate from medical school at Eastern Carolina, which explained why he was doing his third year of surgical residency at a small rural community hospital like Covington instead of at Duke, Wake Forest, or Chapel Hill's university hospitals. He was a kind, handsome, and earnest young man, but a barely competent surgeon. He would likely be relegated to doing nothing but the most routine appendectomies and bunion repairs when he finished his residency and entered private practice. Joanna's heart went out to him as he and his second-year classmate, Hattie Brown, stumbled their way through their elderly patient's surgery.

"Nurse Watson?" Dr. Brown asked timidly. "Should we complete the uterus removal before doing the ovaries, or after?" Hattie Brown was a stout, middle-aged African-American woman, who had put herself through medical school after single-handedly raising three children. "I was thinking we should complete the uterus removal first, then cauterize and tie off all those incisions before proceeding with the ovaries."

Joanna smiled underneath her mask. Joanna could tell that despite her age and unconventional career path, the older woman already had the makings of a very good surgeon. "Yes, Dr. Brown, I think that's exactly the thing to do here. Don't you agree, Shirley?"

Shirley Daniels, perched at her usual spot next to the anesthesia machine, gave only a single nod in response. Shirley was still acting apprehensive around her. Joanna wondered exactly how much the younger nurse knew about her and Harlan.

"Thanks for the advice, Nurse Watson," Dr. Brown said as she began to complete the uterus removal, taking over for the now-trembling Dr. Grenoway completely. He backed against the porcelain wall of the OR, holding his number three scalpel in midair. Dr. Brown took it from him and completed the last few cuts.

"You're most welcome, Dr. Brown," Joanna said, nodding her approval. "You're doing a fine job, by the way. And please, call me Joanna."

"Only if you call me Hattie," Dr. Brown beamed, obviously thrilled at the compliment.

Dr. Grenoway finally shook off his nervous funk and went to assist Dr. Brown in cauterizing their incisions when suddenly, one of Shirley Daniels's many monitors began bleating an alarm.

"Her blood pressure's dropping!" Shirley shouted. "She's already at 72 over 40 and falling fast!"

Dr. Grenoway froze, the cauterizing tool in his hand still smoking and whirring. Joanna reached across Mrs. Small's wide-open abdomen and shut it off. "What do we do, Nurse Watson?" he asked, terrified.

Joanna took over immediately. "Dr. Brown, get the patient two units of blood, stat. Shirley, decrease the amount of anesthesia a bit – that might bring her pressure up. Dr. Grenoway, treat Mrs. Small for systolic shock. Make sure she's not bleeding internally from any unsutured incisions. I'll finish the cauterization myself—"

"But nurses can't do that by themselves – it's against hospital regulations!" Dr. Grenoway protested, yanking the cauterizing tool out of Joanna's reach.

"Screw regulations," Joanna spat back. "I've cauterized plenty of times on plenty of procedures, and I can do it faster than either of you can. We've got to stop all the excess bleeding fast, or we'll lose Mrs. Small for sure."

Dr. Grenoway finally acquiesced and handed Joanna the cauterizing tool. He began the standard OR treatment for systolic shock while Joanna went to work cleaning up all of Mrs. Small's open incisions. Just as she thought she had everything under control, she spotted the cause of Mrs. Small's rapid drop in blood pressure. Someone – Dr. Grenoway, Joanna guessed – had nicked Mrs. Small's aortic artery, and as a result the poor woman was gushing huge amounts of blood into the rear of her abdominal cavity. Joanna was stunned that neither she nor the other two doctors had noticed it before.

"Dr. Brown – Hattie – get Mrs. Small four units of blood. *Now*."

The older woman stared back at her. "But she's only lost one unit so far!"

"*Do it*," Joanna barked, amazed at how authoritarian she sounded. "*Now*. Or Mrs. Small is as good as dead." Dr. Brown obeyed. Joanna somehow managed to stop the artery bleeding with a mix of quick stitches and creative use of the cauterizing tool. Her fingers flew along the elderly woman's abdominal cavity with a dexterity and skill Joanna hadn't known she possessed. Shirley, Dr. Brown, and Dr. Grenoway all watched in awe.

When Joanna finally got the bleeding under control, Mrs. Small's blood pressure began to rise to a more normal level.

"Well done, everyone. We'll need to suction out the excess blood from the abdominal cavity before it clots. Dr. Grenoway, do that, please."

"But suction is *your* responsibility, Nurse!" The young doctor looked close to throwing a temper tantrum right on the OR floor.

"Dr. Grenoway, with all due respect, I don't think you should be going anywhere near a scalpel until further notice," Joanna snapped, her voice cold. "I imagine it was you who nicked the aortal artery and got us in this mess in the first place. Do the suction, or I'll be forced to report your incompetence to your residency director."

Without another word, Dr. Grenoway began the suction.

Chapter Twenty-one

JOANNA UNDRESSED in the locker room in silence. She tried to ignore the fact that Shirley Daniels kept shooting her dirty looks from across the room, but so far it wasn't working.

"You had no right to yell at Dr. Grenoway like that," Shirley snapped.

Joanna slammed her locker shut. "Well, if I hadn't, we would have had a dead patient on our hands. Bottom line, the man's a crummy surgeon. I think the hospital should get rid of him."

Those words cut Shirley to the bone. Joanna saw her wince and shudder at their impact. Now she knew for sure that Shirley and Dr. Grenoway were intimate.

"Dr. Grenoway *is* a good surgeon," Shirley protested. "He's just, well, *distracted* lately."

Joanna chuckled. "By what, pray tell? *You*?" She stood up from her bench and slammed her locker shut. "You do realize that Dr. Grenoway is engaged to be married, don't you?"

Shirley blushed beet-red. "I don't know what you mean," she muttered. But it was obvious from her flushed face and heaving chest that she did.

Joanna put her hands on her hips. "Look, Shirley. I don't have anything against you as a person. I never have. You're a very good nurse-anesthetist, and the hospital is very lucky to have you on staff.

So I don't know why all of a sudden you seem to be in some kind of cutthroat competition with me. Over what, I have no idea. Surely not my job. I work even longer hours than you do."

Shirley ground her teeth loud enough for Joanna to hear. "Let's just say there's something around the hospital that we both want, and that we're both willing to do anything to get," she chirped. "And I do mean *anything*." With that, she turned on her heel and marched out of the locker room.

Joanna watched her go, dumbfounded. Was the thing that they both wanted Harlan? And if so, what exactly was Shirley willing to do to get him and keep him all to herself?

Joanna didn't want to think about that right now. All she did want was to take a shower to help clear her head.

Joanna stepped into the stall, turned the shower knob all the way to "HOT", and stood under the scalding stream for a full minute, oblivious to the screaming nerve endings in her back. She needed the hot water to help relax the heavy tension and fatigue that was knotting her neck and arm muscles.

Joanna stood under the scorching hot water for another thirty seconds, then slowly added some cold water until the temperature was more tolerable. She scrubbed, soaped, and shampooed, knowing full well she was due back in the OR in less than half an hour for yet another complex operation – this time, a hernia repair on a morbidly obese teenage patient, Todd Palmetto. Todd's young age, extreme obesity, and history of heart murmur would make this operation even more difficult to manage than Mrs. Small's. And the last thing she needed right now was to worry about whether the nurse-anesthetist she worked with every day had designs on the man she was in love with.

Wait a minute – she was *in love* with Harlan? No, that couldn't possibly be true. Not at all.

Could it?

She stood back up under the showerhead and turned the taps all the way over to "COLD." It was going to take a lot of icy water to bring her back to earth after such a frightening thought.

Nothing was more frightening to her than the thought of losing Harlan forever. Nothing.

Joanna know then and there she had to make one last-ditch effort to bring Harlan back into her life.

Now calm, cool, and relaxed, Joanna rinsed off, got out of the shower, dressed, and headed for Hospital Administration.

*****

"That's impossible!" Joseph Middleton, president and chief executive officer of Covington Community Hospital, barked when Joanna suggested that Harlan be brought back from suspension. "He's injured, and by his own clumsy hand too!"

"I'm not asking that he actually *perform* surgery until his hand heals," Joanna replied, keeping her voice calm. "But given what happened in the OR with Mrs. Small, I believe it is absolutely imperative that an experienced attending surgeon be present while those two green residents are doing the bulk of the work. Otherwise, you are putting Covington's patients at unnecessary risk. Which of course increases the hospital's potential liability."

Joanna knew from experience that curmudgeon hospital administrators like Middleton generally only responded to terms like "risk" and "liability."

Middleton chewed the end of his expensive fountain pen for a moment. "I hear what you're saying, Joanna, I really do. But I can't be giving anyone the idea that I don't discipline surgeons when they screw up royally. And Wilkinson screwed up *very* royally."

"Don't you think it's punishment enough for any surgeon to be rendered unable to operate?" Joanna countered. "He might never be able to hold a scalpel again if too much scar tissue forms in the wound. And even if his hand heals completely, he'll still be unable to fully operate for at least a month, maybe two." Joanna tried hard not to sound too eager. Even if she was only doing this a ploy to melt the hard ass-S.O.B. surgeon's heart, Joanna knew she had to come across to Middleton as making the suggestion because it was in the best interest of patients, not Harlan's. And certainly not her own.

"We don't want what happened during Mrs. Small's operation to happen again," she went on. "Fortunately we were able to save her, but we might not be so lucky next time. You don't want to expose your hospital to any unnecessary *liability*, do you?"

Middleton chewed his expensive pen again. "Joanna, I don't think I need to remind you that what happened during Mrs. Small's operation, for all intents and purposes, *did not* happen. Officially speaking, anyway." Joanna could tell that the seasoned old administrator was nervous. "You know our liability insurance premiums are high enough as it is."

"Of course, sir," Joanna said, smiling sweetly. "It *did not* happen, officially speaking. But *unofficially* speaking, I think it would be prudent to have an attending surgeon on hand for all operations. We can never be too careful."

Middleton set down his fountain pen and paused to think. "Well, Joanna, I suppose you're right. I'll see what I can do to bring Dr. Wilkinson back right away. But he'd still technically be on suspension, and I'd only bring him back as a consultant, on half-pay."

"Thank you, sir," Joanna beamed. "I'm sure the patients will appreciate knowing their surgical care is given under Dr. Wilkinson's expert supervision. Do you think you could get him back in time for Todd Palmetto's hernia operation? That's scheduled in about half an hour, and it's quite risky given Mr. Palmetto's – ahem – large size."

Middleton got up from his desk and went to stare out his large picture window. "Well, I'll have him paged, but Wilkinson left here a couple of hours ago in an absolute tizzy, and I don't mean just about being put on suspension. Seems he's pretty angry with *you* especially. Can you tell me anything about that, Joanna?"

Joanna swallowed hard. "I'm afraid I can't, sir. I haven't the slightest idea why Dr. Wilkinson would be angry with me," she lied.

"Well, I suggest you find out why as soon as he gets here," Joseph ordered. "I can't afford to have the guy mad at this hospital's best nurse, no matter how much of an arrogant S.O.B. he might be."

"I will," Joanna said, stifling a chuckle. Maybe there was hope for her and Harlan after all.

Chapter Twenty-two

TWENTY MINUTES later, Joanna was at the scrub trough, elbow-deep in PhisoDerm suds when Shirley Daniels burst into the room.

"What a load of bullshit!" the nurse-anesthetist screamed. "What a load of fucking bullshit."

Joanna smiled to herself. She had a pretty good idea what had Shirley so upset, but she wasn't about to give away what she knew. "What's the matter, Shirley?"

"Darth Vader is coming back! He's going to supervise the Todd Palmetto operation!" Shirley rolled up her sleeves and joined Joanna at the scrub trough.

"Well, well, well," Joanna sang. "Looks like we'll both get a chance to see Dr. Wilkinson in action again. I'm sure you're as excited about it as I am." Joanna rinsed off and started pulling on her surgical mask and overgown, and she couldn't help but notice that Shirley was purple with rage.

"Pshaw," Shirley scoffed, and set herself to scrubbing. Joanna left her covered in PhisoDerm and went into the OR to start preparing the instrument trays.

She'd won this round.

Joanna was arranging rows of sterile scalpels on the main instrument table when Harlan came into the OR, already gowned and masked. "Greetings, Watson," he said gruffly, not even meeting her eyes.

"Good evening, Dr. Wilkinson. We're all so pleased you could join us for Mr. Palmetto's operation." Joanna kept her gaze focused on the surgical trays.

"Like hell you are," Harlan seethed. "That cranky nurse-anesthetist practically drowned me in suds at the scrub trough. Among other things."

Joanna smiled underneath her mask. "Shirley's just overtired, is all. She's been pulling double and triple shifts all week. Two of the other anesthetists quit, you know." Joanna was careful not to mention they'd both quit because of him.

Harlan did not comment on this. "If this were any kind of hospital, you'd have an MD-level anesthesiologist running the gas during operations, not a two-bit nurse."

Joanna cleared her throat. "I'm sure you're well aware that small rural hospitals can't afford to have full-time anesthesiologists on staff, Dr. Wilkinson."

"I'm aware that small rural hospitals can't afford to have a lot of things" Harlan's ice-blue eyes bore into Joanna. Try as she might, she couldn't look away from them.

Joanna felt her cheeks burn as Harlan broke off his gaze. He turned his back on Joanna and went to read Todd Palmetto's patient history.

Joanna finished counting scalpels and turned to face him. "Harlan, about what happened the other day. I'm sorry if what I did upset you, but you have to understand that I felt you weren't being honest with me. And if you want to talk more about what Bob was suggesting—"

He held up his hand. "Watson, there won't be any further discussion about what happened back in the parking lot." Harlan's voice was austere, businesslike. "I mean it. Case closed." The fire that had once burned in his blue eyes at Joanna's very presence had vanished.

"What happened in the parking lot?" Shirley chirped. She apparently had slipped into the room unnoticed; there was no telling how much of their conversation she'd overheard.

"Nothing," Joanna stammered. "Dr. Wilkinson and I were having a – a political disagreement."

"Riiiiiight," Shirley said. She glanced from Harlan to Joanna, then back to Harlan, and chuckled. "A *political* disagreement, sure. Whatever you say."

"Daniels, I'd appreciate it if you kept the running commentary to a minimum," Harlan barked. Joanna gave him a warning look, but he ignored her. "It's bad enough that I'm stuck with you as my anesthetist, since apparently everyone else has quit."

"I'll quit too if you don't watch your mouth," Shirley shot back. Her tone was harsh, but her facial expression was sultry and flirtatious, almost as if she were playing hard-to-get.

Harlan rolled his eyes and ignored her. The tension in the OR hung so thick you could spear it with a fork. "Where the hell's this hernia patient, anyway?" Harlan barked. "And where are my two residents, who probably can't even slice butter properly, let alone a person?"

As if on cue, Dr. Brown and Dr. Grenoway appeared, already gowned and masked. Three more masked orderlies followed them, all pushing a gurney that held the largest person Joanna had ever seen. Todd Palmetto was already partially sedated. The folds of his fatty flesh spilled over the sides of the gurney like so much Jell-O. He was more than half asleep on pre-op meds, and his mouth hung open, dripping with two very long, iridescent cords of drool. Joanna guessed he had to weigh at least four hundred pounds. Small wonder the poor boy had a hernia.

"Is this the patient?" Harlan said with noticeable distaste.

"Yes, sir," Dr. Grenoway replied, eager to impress the gruff attending surgeon. "He has a strangulated hiatal hernia which has currently wrapped itself around both the large intestine and part of the aortal artery, causing significant pain and digestive problems, not to mention significant circulatory risks. Adding to the regular potential complications, he's—"

"Morbidly obese," Harlan finished. "Yes, I can see that, Greno-way. Perhaps one of you two young punks can tell me how you plan to operate on this poor guy." He nodded towards Dr. Brown.

"With all due respect, Doctor, I'm older than you," Hattie Brown said.

"It was a figure of speech," Harlan said, softening his tone a little. "Tell me your game plan, Dr. Brown."

The stout middle-aged woman arranged herself at the head of Todd Palmetto's gurney as if preparing for battle. "Well, once he's under anesthesia, I thought we would start by making four incisions in the lower abdomen—"

"Wrong answer," Harlan cut her off. "You forgot to address proper anesthesia for a morbidly obese person. Isn't that right, Daniels?"

Shirley nodded, obviously pleased Harlan was paying her some attention.

"Daniels, why don't you inform old Dr. Brown here about the importance of proper anesthesia?" Harlan's tone was patronizing, but Shirley showed no outward sign of offense.

"Administering anesthesia to morbidly obese persons requires adjustments in dosage, as well as increased monitoring of blood pressure and blood oxygen levels," Shirley said matter-of-factly. "I've already made the calculations for increasing Mr. Palmetto's dosage by eighteen percent, and I have additional monitors in place for checking his blood oxygen levels as well."

"Good, Daniels. Maybe you're competent after all." Shirley beamed.

Harlan turned back to the two residents. "Good surgeons always consult their anesthesiologists – or in this case, *nurse-anesthetists* – before making any cuts. Do you know who else good surgeons consult first?"

Both residents shrugged.

"The lead OR nurse. Right, Watson?"

Joanna nodded. "I've already briefed the residents, Harlan. Two hours ago. It's a pretty standard hernia, caused by the pressure and strain of extreme obesity."

"Watson, please do not use my first name in the OR. That is highly unprofessional. Isn't that right, everyone?"

Shirley clucked. Dr. Brown and Dr. Grenoway exchanged glances, but said nothing.

Joanna felt herself flush. "Pardon me, *Doctor* Wilkinson," she cooed. "Since you're so cavalier about how you address your nurses, I wasn't aware you were so sensitive about your own name." A more than witty comeback, considering the circumstances. Joanna smiled to herself.

Harlan didn't miss a beat. "Well, if you had taken the time to read Mr. Palmetto's MRI report more closely, *Ms.* Watson, you would have seen that his hernia was not caused by his obesity, but by a botched lap-band surgery. By the looks of it, he got it done on the cheap in Mexico."

"Mexico?" Dr. Grenoway was impressed. "How can you tell?"

Harlan pulled an MRI film out of Todd Palmetto's file and hooked it onto the light box. "Here," he said, pointing to a barely visible gray line on the mottled gray image of Todd's digestive tract. "That's the electronic signature of the Inamedic 2000 Lap-Band, a low-tech precursor to today's lap-band devices. The Inamedic 2000 has been illegal in the United States for almost ten years due to its high complication rate. You're getting a nice, up-close-and-personal look at one of those complications right now. The only place you can get one of these babies put in your belly anymore is in rural Mexico. Not pretty, is it?"

Joanna was stunned. She'd had no idea what looked like a simple hernia was really a botched weight-loss operation. Harlan had managed to one-up her once again.

"Watson, as the senior nurse in this OR, I expect you to set a proper example for others. *All* others, even inexperienced residents, who are still medical doctors and therefore always outrank you." Harlan's tone was vicious and cutting. Girding herself with resolve, Joanna refused to give him the satisfaction of unnerving her in public.

"My mistake, Doctor," she said flatly. "It won't happen again."

And it wouldn't. From that moment of humiliation, Joanna decided she was through with Dr. Harlan Wilkinson, once and for all.

Chapter Twenty-three

JOANNA WAS crashed out on an unmade cot in the residents' quarters after nearly sixteen straight hours of OR duty when she felt someone poke her in the shoulder.

"Go 'way," she moaned, and pulled the paper-thin cot pillow over her head. "Sleeping."

The poking turned into violent shaking. "Mmmmpph," Joanna growled, and burrowed herself underneath the rough cotton coverlet.

Suddenly, Joanna found herself on the floor. Someone had overturned her cot. She rubbed her sleep-crusty eyes and looked up. Maryam Malone stood over her, arms folded and mouth set in a hard line. "Joanna, get up."

Joanna looked at her watch. It was eight thirty a.m., which meant she'd only managed to get about four hours of sleep. "Please, Maryam. I'm not due back in the Surgery department until noon. Leave me alone."

"Joseph Middleton wants to see you in his office right away." Maryam grabbed Joanna's right arm and dragged her to her feet.

Joanna stretched, trying in vain to loosen the kinks in her back and neck. "Why?"

"I don't know," Maryam sighed. "But he sounded pretty impatient."

"All right. Just let me get a shower and change my scrubs."

"Actually, Joanna, there's no time for that," Maryam said. "Mr. Middleton wants to see you immediately."

Joanna's jaw dropped. "But I – I'm dirty, and sweaty, and – I look like a street hag!"

Maryam took a set of fresh scrubs out of the closet and handed them to her. "Put these on, and just put a paper scrub cap over your hair. I'll stall Middleton long enough for you to change, but you better be in his office in five minutes, or believe me, he'll be mad enough to spit nails."

Maryam left.

As Joanna tugged on the fresh scrubs, a hundred thoughts coursed through her mind. What had she done wrong? She knew that recommending Dr. Wilkinson be pulled back from suspension had been the right decision medically. Even if he did make everyone who worked under him miserable, Harlan always put patients' needs for the best possible care above all. No matter how irrational or obstinate an administrator Joseph Middleton was, surely he couldn't find fault with Joanna for that. There must be something else.

Joanna tucked her sleep-mangled hair under a paper scrub cap and set out for the hallway. Just as she was crossing the threshold of the dorm, however, a terrible possibility emerged. What exactly had Shirley Daniels overheard between Joanna and Harlan the night before? Shirley had been suspicious of Joanna's relationship with the ill-mannered surgeon even before walking in on their heated argument. There was no telling what the younger nurse knew now. Joanna had never known the nurse-anesthetist to be malicious. But fraternizing between doctors and nurses on staff was against hospital policy. Did Shirley take Harlan's insults and mistreatment in the OR personally enough to report his illicit romance with Joanna out of revenge?

Or worse yet, did Shirley want Harlan all to herself?

There was only one way to find out. Joanna had always been adept at handling herself under pressure, and today wouldn't be any different. She stood up tall and marched down the corridor to Joseph Middleton's office.

*****

"Joanna, I don't like dealing with this kind of thing on the job, so I'll get right to the point. Joseph Middleton's voice was chill and hollow. "Are you sleeping with Dr. Harlan Wilkinson?"

Joanna felt the bottom drop out of her stomach. "Excuse me?"

Middleton's mouth was a thin hard line. "Just answer the question."

"Mr. Middleton, if you don't mind, I am not comfortable discussing my private life with you."

The elderly man sighed. "My apologies, Joanna. I wouldn't normally think to ask you questions that invaded your privacy, but I received some rather disturbing calls this morning that leave me no choice."

Joanna sucked in a mouthful of air. "What do you mean, *disturbing* calls?"

Middleton got up from his leatherbacked chair and began to pace the room. "This morning I received two calls. One from an attorney, claiming to represent your former husband, Mr. Robert Watson. That attorney claims that you are engaging in an inappropriate sexual relationship with Dr. Robert Wilkinson – who, I might remind you, is also your direct supervisor."

Joanna went pale as paper. "That – that's not true," she sputtered. Her voice came out as a squeak. She wasn't exactly lying, either. As far as she knew, her sexual relationship with Harlan *was* over.

"Well, I want to believe you, Joanna. As I'm sure you know, intimate relationships between unmarried attending physicians and subordinates are prohibited by hospital policy. I called Wilkinson in here myself this morning and asked him if there was any truth to the allegations, and he vehemently denied it. That and your own word would have been enough for me to dismiss the attorney's claim as malicious and unfounded under normal circumstances. But shortly after I spoke to Wilkinson, I received a second, more disturbing call on the same subject – this time, from one of our own hospital staff. I'll refrain from saying who."

Joanna looked down at the floor. It was as she feared – the second call had to have been from Shirley Daniels. There was no other explanation. "What did this other person say?"

"This staff person alleged that she – or he – overheard a conversation between yourself and Wilkinson in the OR that can only be described as a lover's spat. Is this true, Joanna?"

It took a moment before Joanna could reply. Her jaw seemed to be wired shut. After much effort, she spoke. "No. It's absolutely untrue," she said, feeling her stomach tie itself into knots at the lie. "What this – person overheard, he or she must certainly have misinterpreted the conversation. I am sure if you confront Dr. Wilkinson on the topic, he will say the same."

Middleton collapsed back into his heavy upholstered chair. "I've left a message for Wilkinson to see me about this latest allegation, but he hasn't responded yet. If he responds the way you say he will, I will consider the matter closed. If not, I will be forced to launch an investigation, per policy on this sensitive kind of matter. It's nothing personal against you of course, Joanna – you're just about the best nurse I've got, and I'd hate to lose you over something trivial like this. But policy is policy, and I have to adhere to it, like it or not. I hope you understand." The old man folded his hands onto his parchment desk blotter.

"Of course, sir." Joanna's knees had gone to jelly. She suddenly felt very faint.

"Are you all right, Joanna? You're very pale."

"Fine, sir. Just very tired after so many hours on duty. With your permission, I'd like to return to the dormitory for some rest before I go back into the OR at noon."

"Permission granted, of course," the old man said, adding some much-needed cheer to his voice. "Rest up, Joanna. We need you to be at your best."

"I know," she muttered. "Thank you, Mr. Middleton, for having faith in me." Joanna nodded her leave and headed down the corridor back to the dormitory, dragging her feet in shame all the way.

*****

Shirley Daniels was furious.

She paced the length of her living room, practically wearing a trough into her shag carpeting. All the time and effort she'd spent to make herself into the most sexually desirable woman in Statesville had failed.

She had just failed to seduce Dr. Harlan Wilkinson.

Shirley didn't understand it. Where had she gone wrong?

She'd dropped tons of hints in the OR – all of which Harlan either rebuffed or ignored. She'd sauntered up to him in the men's locker room post-op, even flashed him a little boob – nothing. He'd told her to leave him the hell alone. And if she didn't, he promised to report her to Human Resources for sexual harassment.

Who the hell did that man think he was, anyway? Because Shirley knew for a fact that Harlan and Joanna had been banging each other on hospital time, too. What a hypocrite he was for threatening *her*!

Well, she'd show him. She'd show Harlan and Joanna what happened when they messed with the sexiest woman in town.

She'd make sure neither one of them would be able to show their faces in public ever again. And while she was making the rounds around town last night, she'd met just the man to help her do just that.

Bob Watson, Joanna's ex-husband.

And Bob had exactly the kind of information that would help Shirley get the kind of revenge she wanted.

*****

At just past eleven, Joanna sat in the hospital break room, eating some microwaved Ramen noodles and corn chips she'd bought from one of the vending machines. She'd showered and freshened up, and wore a fresh set of scrubs. Lying to Mr. Middleton about the nature of her relationship with Dr. Harlan Wilkinson weighed heavily on Joanna's shoulders.

True, she and Harlan technically weren't lovers. Not anymore, anyway. But even as Joanna stiffened her resolve to never allow herself to fall under Harlan Wilkinson's seductive spell again, she would be lying if she said she still wasn't wildly attracted to him. In fact, she was probably more attracted to him now than ever.

Joanna munched her pathetic breakfast and considered her increasingly desperate situation. Would Harlan back up her story when Middleton confronted him for the second time? She expected he would, but knowing that he would publicly deny ever having feelings for her a *second* time only caused her even more pain. What would be the harm in Joseph Middleton knowing the truth about their liaisons?

What harm, indeed. Both Joanna and Harlan could be booted from their jobs, publicly humiliated, and worse.

Joanna spent the last dollar she had in her purse to buy a Red Bull energy drink from the vending machine. She needed energy to face the many demons bearing down at her today. Joanna took the thin silver can from the machine, popped the top, and prepared to down the foul-tasting stuff when a gruff voice just behind her made her freeze.

"That junk is very bad for your stomach lining, Joanna. Not to mention the heart."

Joanna turned on her heel and found Harlan staring back at her. He was in fresh green scrubs, well-worn Airwalk sneakers, and was unshaven. A tight scrub cap sat askew on his head.

In short, he looked amazing. Joanna had to steady herself as the temperature of her crotch soared skyward. "Red Bull is perfectly safe to drink," she retorted, and guzzled the can's entire contents in one gulp as if to prove herself right. After swallowing, a huge, vibrating belch emanated from her mouth before she had a chance to stifle it. Harlan winced, then gave her a lopsided grin.

"Nice belch," he said.

Joanna tossed the empty into the recycling bin. "Well, I need *something* to keep me awake." Joanna cut a sidelong glance over at Harlan, then skipped right past him, head held high. She would not give him any opportunities to get the upper hand on her today.

Famous last words.

Chapter Twenty-four

WHEN JOANNA reported for duty at noon, she was surprised to find the patient intake bin empty of files. The pre-op ward was strangely deserted, and all the Recovery beds were empty, too.

Joanna marched straight to Maryam Malone's desk for an explanation. "Maryam, where did all the patient files go?"

Maryam bit her lip. "We have a bit of a situation."

"What situation is that?"

Maryam motioned for Joanna to sit down. "The Surgery department here has been shut down by the state medical board of North Carolina until further notice."

Joanna stared back at the older nurse, mouth agape. "Shut *down*? But why?"

Maryam shook her head. "Nobody knows, and Middleton and the rest of Administration aren't talking."

Joanna blew out a heavy breath of air. "When did this happen?"

"The state inspector just showed up about half an hour ago, while you were having your breakfast," Maryam explained. "He ordered the entire Surgery department shut down immediately, and had all our cases transferred, mostly to St. Michael's over in Durham. A few of the more serious ones just got airlifted to University Hospital in Raleigh. The last ones left just before you got down here. That's all I know."

Harlan burst into Maryam's cubicle. "Where the hell are all my patients?"

Maryam repeated her story for Harlan's benefit, then sighed. "In all my years, I've never once had a department shut down by a state inspector that was under *my* supervision," she said. "Where did I go wrong? I must be getting too old for this job."

"Whatever caused this, Maryam, I'm sure it was just a big misunderstanding," Joanna offered, trying to sound upbeat. She glanced over at Harlan, and saw that his face had turned an alarming shade of gray.

"Excuse me, ladies," he muttered, and went tottering down the hall.

Maryam clucked. "I'm willing to bet *he* knows something," she said, jerking her head in Harlan's direction. "Serves him right if he's in some kind of trouble with the state review board, the jerk."

Joanna worked hard to keep her voice steady. "What makes you think *he* knows something?" Joanna asked innocently. But the pained expression on Harlan's face a moment ago had been like a flashing neon sign. "You don't think this has to do with him cutting himself in the OR, does it?"

Maryam shook her head. "No, I don't believe the state would shut the entire Surgery department down just for something like that. Whatever the real reason is, I'll try to find out. And as soon as I know, I'll tell you. In the meantime, you should probably just go home and get some rest, Joanna. I can keep an eye on things here by myself."

Joanna nodded, fiddling with her hands. She'd needed to get back to her condo and collect her thoughts.

*****

Joanna had gathered up her belongings and was headed out to her car, still in her duty scrubs, when she encountered Harlan in the hospital parking garage. Her stomach lurched when she saw him, but not in a bad way. More like in an *arousing* kind of way.

Harlan had changed out of his scrubs into a well-worn pair of jeans and a beige golf shirt. He was leaning against the concrete half-wall at the far end of the parking garage, staring out across the front lawn of the hospital at the shadowy lines of the Blue Ridge Mountains in the distance. He seemed transfixed by the view, almost in a trance. Joanna was almost afraid to approach him, but the warming sensation in her belly and groin involuntarily pulled her body towards his.

Joanna stopped short about a foot away from Harlan. He didn't seem to notice her approach. She studied his neck and back, the contours of his shoulders, the firm curve of his buttocks. Her gaze ran all the way down his backside to his bare ankles – his feet were shoved, sockless, into his worn sneakers – and back up again until her eyes rested on the nape of his neck. She inspected each and every one of the short, sandy wisps of hair along the bottom of his hairline, saw how they whorled into a perfect arrow that pointed down to the exact center of his shoulderblades. She gazed intently at the back of each of his earlobes, saw how they both had tiny dimples in them, how they were both attached to the sides of his neck. For some crazy reason she felt like encasing both of those earlobes between her lips, felt like sucking them, felt like running her tongue around and around the grooves and arches of his ears. Joanna became lost in the imagined sensations Harlan's body inspired in her, and soon the line between what was imaginary and what was real became blurred. His mere presence caused Joanna's nether parts to swell, to moisten, to scream for his touch, his lips, his tongue. A mewling whimper escaped Joanna's throat as she stood lost in the pleasures of her fantasy.

Harlan spun around. "Joanna," he said, his voice low, almost like velvet. "I—I didn't know you were here."

Joanna froze. She couldn't speak. She couldn't even breathe.

"Joanna, all you all right?"

She managed a small nod. To her surprise, Harlan took her right hand into his left one, and stroked the inside of her palm. The feel of his touch against her skin was like a million tiny bonfires filling every pore of her being.

"Joanna, I've been less than honest with you. With everyone, in fact." Harlan let go of her hand and turned back away from her to stare at the mountains again.

Joanna placed a timid hand on his shoulder. The feel of his body underneath her fingers sent pulsing waves of electricity through her body all the way down to her feet. "What do you mean?"

Harlan's left hand – the uninjured one – gripped the rusty steel bar fastened to the top of the concrete half-wall that was the only thing separating him from a fall to the hospital's concrete driveway below.

Harlan turned around again, taking her hand off his shoulder and raising it to his lips. He kissed the back of her hand, kissed each of her knuckles, and then, one by one, sucked each and every one of her fingers. Joanna felt her knees buckle out from under her. She started to fall, and Harlan caught her up in his arms.

Harlan's mouth seized upon hers. They kissed for a full minute before Joanna broke away from him, her heart pounding between her ears, her head spinning at mach velocity.

"We can't do this," she gasped, leaning against the cold concrete wall. "Not here, anyway."

"Why not?" Harlan moved to kiss her again.

Joanna backed away. "Someone will see us!"

Harlan touched the side of her face. He ran his fingertips across her cheekbone, along her jaw. His touch was like a sergeant's command. Whatever part of her he caressed ordered her to submit to his will. It was all she could do for her mind to disobey the sensual directives of her body. "So what if they do?" he asked.

"You should already know the answer to that," Joanna shot back. "Too many people are asking too many questions about us. It will only come back to haunt us both if anyone knows."

"Knows what? Why do you care? We haven't done anything wrong, Joanna. Well, maybe I have, but—" Harlan trailed off, stared down at the asphalt.

"But what? What do you mean?" Joanna put her index finger under Harlan's chin, raised his head and forced him to look her in the eyes. "What have you done wrong, Harlan?"

"Joanna, do you have a few hours to spare? Because that's at least as long as it will take to tell you about all the wrong that I have done."

Chapter Twenty-five

"WHERE ARE you taking me?" Joanna asked as Harlan drove her in his car – a silver Jaguar convertible – along a deserted mountain road. He'd kept the top up so far, something Joanna was thankful for given the early-spring chill. Her Honda was still back at the hospital garage.

"Somewhere where nobody will see us. That's what you want, right?"

"Yes," she said, examining her hands. They were shaking.

"Middleton talked to you too, didn't he?" Harlan shifted gears and accelerated up a steep grade, never once taking his eyes off the road.

"Yes, he did."

"It seems a lot of people are talking about us, Joanna. Maybe you could explain why."

Joanna looked down at her hands again. Now they were vibrating. She interlaced her fingers and made a double fist, clenching it into the hollow of her lap in a vain attempt to settle her buzzing body down. "I don't know what you mean."

"Well, first, somebody on staff at the hospital says we're banging each other at work against hospital policy – which, technically we are. And now your ex-husband's lawyer calls the hospital and says the same thing. What's your ex-husband got to do with hospital regulations, anyway?"

"I have no idea," she replied. And it was the truth.

"Well, something fishy is definitely going on," Harlan said. He shifted gears and started to slow the car.

"Why are you slowing down?" Joanna asked, alarmed.

"We're getting close to my house." Harlan turned left sharply onto an unmarked gravel driveway almost hidden by trees, kudzu, and undergrowth. He followed its meandering, uneven path for almost a mile up the mountainside, until they came upon a small, saltbox-style A-frame lodge that jutted itself partway off a cliff. A deep, narrow ravine separated the house from the driveway. Joanna noticed that the entire eastern wall of the house – the part that seemed seconds away from falling down the mountainside – was made almost entirely of glass. A long wooden catwalk with six-foot-high railings led across the ravine and up to the house. The place was all sharp angles, invisible foundation, and improbable location – not unlike Dr. Harlan Wilkinson himself.

"This is it, Joanna. What do you think?"

"It's. . .interesting," was the only comment Joanna could manage.

"And remote," he finished. "That's what I like most about it. Nobody knows it's up here except my housekeeper. The electricity runs on a generator, and I have well water. So no public utilities. I take my garbage down the mountain – or rather, my housekeeper does— twice a week, so no trash service to know that it's here. My mail doesn't come here, either. My cell phone gets a signal up here most of the time, except when it storms, but there's no land line telephone service up this high. It's the utmost in privacy."

"I see," Joanna said, wondering why on earth Harlan would want to live in such utter isolation from the world. "Did you build it yourself?"

"No, I bought it several years ago from some crazy survivalist guy," Harlan explained. "He *did* build it himself. Apparently he worked as an architect before he became a crazy survivalist. He only lived in it for a year, then left it vacant."

"Uh huh," Joanna said, chuckling. "Apparently he didn't survive out here very long, then."

"Nope, he fell down the mountainside, broke his leg in three places, and had to go move in with his daughter in Raleigh." He laughed. "I used to come down here from Boston once or twice a year for hunting trips, but when I took the job at Covington – well, it made for a perfect full-time home." Harlan walked down the catwalk towards the front door, and Joanna followed him inside.

The view from the lodge's floor-to-ceiling glass wall was magnificent. The entire Blue Ridge range was visible from this altitude, and all the colors of a North Carolina mountain spring laid themselves out across every hill and valley. Joanna wasn't sure, but she thought she could see all the way to the Tennessee state line. "It's a wonderful view," she breathed, captivated.

"That's exactly why I bought the place," Harlan said.

Harlan squeezed her shoulders hard, bringing Joanna partially out of her reverie. "Joanna, if we make love here, nobody at work will ever know. I promise you."

"I—" Joanna split away from him, bit at her thumbnail like a gawky girl. "I don't know, Harlan. I think there's something strange going on. There are people who don't want to see us happy together." Like Shirley Daniels. Like her ex-husband.

"Do you really care what anybody else thinks?" Harlan folded his arms across his broad chest, cocked his head to one side. "Tell me the truth."

"No, I don't. But that doesn't change the facts at hand." Joanna's breathing came in hot, heavy spurts. Her upper body felt heavy and warm, her nether parts were molten steel. Her nipples were quartz crystals that threatened to shred the front of her thin cotton scrub blouse. Joanna's body was ready to have sex with this man, certainly. But her mind wasn't. Her heart wasn't, either. Her mind was too full of questions, her heart too full of doubts. What was he hiding from her? What wrongs had he done, and did he really intend to tell her about them?

"Penny for your thoughts," Harlan whispered, only inches away from her ear. She was so lost in her spiraling thoughts that he had slid his strong arms around her waist without her even noticing.

This man had too much power over her, far too much.

"Are you going to tell me all the things you've done wrong?" she asked, still not quite ready to pull herself from his embrace.

"I'll tell you after we have sex," he whispered, nibbling at her ear. "*While* we have sex, if you prefer."

As tantalizing as Harlan's suggestion was, Joanna knew it was impossible. She broke away from him, crossed to the far side of the room. "I need you to tell me everything first," she said. "*All* of it. Tell me everything, or there won't ever be anything between us. We have to be honest with each other, Harlan."

Harlan looked wounded. "Why are you so insistent that I tell you everything, Joanna? I haven't made that demand of you."

Joanna took a deep breath before replying. "I want to know what it is that makes you so angry and mean all the time."

Harlan's eyes flew wide. "Excuse me?"

"That's right," Joanna said, triumphant. "You're mean."

"No, I'm not."

"Please. Have you ever listened to yourself in the OR? You give new meaning to the word arrogant." Joanna flopped down in one of the lodge's many beanbag-style chairs. "Most of my fellow nurses have quit rather than put up with you. You're mean, and rude, and obnoxious, and foul-mouthed, and—"

"An S.O.B.?" To Joanna's surprise, Harlan was smiling.

"Yes, you're definitely an S.O.B. You know what the other nurses call you behind your back?"

Harlan's grin widened. "I can only imagine. What?"

"Darth Vader."

Joanna expected Harlan to be angry at this, but he just laughed. "Actually, I'm probably closer to Palpatine."

Joanna's *Star Wars* knowledge didn't include anyone named Palpatine. "Which one's Palpatine?"

"You know, the Emperor. He's the one with the melted face in *Return of the Jedi*."

"Oh," Joanna muttered, embarrassed. "Right." Dr. Harlan Wilkinson had one-upped her once again.

"Did *you* ever call me Darth Vader, Joanna?"

Joanna smirked a little. "Actually, I thought 'Darth Vader' was too kind a nickname for you. You remind me more of Attila the Hun."

"Fair enough. I've never been very sociable, even when I was a kid," Harlan said, sitting down in the beanbag chair opposite Joanna.

"It shows," Joanna remarked.

"Look Joanna, if you really want to hear what I have to say, you'll need to keep the sarcastic comments to a minimum. I haven't made many demands of you—"

"I beg to differ on that. You've made *plenty* of demands, Harlan. Would you like me to list them for you?"

Harlan sighed. "Fine. Point taken." He walked back over to her. In a single, brilliant move, Harlan straddled her, leaning over so that his bulging crotch was right on top of her bosom. He took hold of her face with his left hand, drawing it close to his, millimeters away from a kiss. But instead of kissing her, he said, "Promise me something, Joanna. Please."

"What?" Joanna could feel his hot breath against her cheeks, her forehead, her neck. With every tickle of his breathing on her skin, her desire for him intensified.

"When I'm done telling this story, let me make love to you."

Joanna smiled. But she didn't answer. Joanna liked the idea of holding Harlan at bay. It made her feel powerful.

"Let me put it in nicer terms, then," Harlan said. "Please, Joanna, let me make love to you," he begged. "The wait is absolutely killing me."

"We'll see," Joanna said, giving Harlan a gentle shove that sent him toppling onto the floor. "Now tell me about all the bad things you've done."

Chapter Twenty-six

HARLAN PULLED a longneck Michelob from his kitchen's glossy black Sub Zero fridge and took a long, slow sip. "All right, Joanna. Here's my story. And when it gets really ugly, disgusting, and horrible to listen to, just remember – you asked for it."

"Actually, *you're* the one who brought up your deep, dark past in the first place," Joanna corrected. "But I know now you only wanted to use it to seduce me."

"Guilty as charged." Harlan finished the beer, then erupted in a loud burp. "There. That's payback for the Red Bull in the break room this morning."

"My burp was much better." Joanna settled deeper into her beanbag chair. "More ladylike, anyway. How about bringing me one of those?" she asked, pointing at his already-guzzled Michelob. He pulled another out of the fridge and tossed it at her from behind the galley kitchen's half-wall. She caught it in her right hand effortlessly.

"Nice catch," Harlan observed. He pulled another beer out of the Sub Zero, popped off the cap, and downed almost half of it in one swallow. "With those reflexes, you could play in the majors."

"I played softball in high school. Center field. By the way, Harlan, you're stalling."

"Right." He inhaled the remains of his second beer in as many minutes, and tossed both empties into the trash. He pulled a ladder-backed chair from the dinette set, and straddled it backwards, chinning the chair's top rung. "I told you that I did some work with Doctors Without Borders, right?"

"Yes. You nailed the woman who later became your wife while on assignment in the Sudan, as I recall." Joanna shook her head and sighed. Harlan had to be the only physician on the planet who would use a Nobel-Prize-winning aid group for sexual purposes.

"You have a good memory. I like that in a woman." Harlan gave her a suggestive look; Joanna ignored it. "I loved the time I spent in Doctors Without Borders. Helping people who desperately needed help gave me self-worth and confidence that I'd never known before." Harlan paused. A look of pain briefly crossed his chiseled features, then disappeared. "You see, I was a quiet kid. An introvert, really. I liked to read and fiddle around in my room with my chemistry set and Tinkertoys. I liked making messes and building things, preferably alone. I never had many friends. Not because I couldn't make them, but because I usually had more fun playing by myself. Playing with other kids meant you had to share, meant you had to compromise. I don't like to compromise. Never have."

"I've noticed that," Joanna chirped.

Harlan blinked. "I consider my inflexibility a strength, frankly."

Joanna rolled her eyes. "You're stalling again, Harlan. I haven't got all day, you know."

Harlan got up from his chair so fast he knocked it over. He began to pace up and down the room. "I first met Emma Swanson in 1993. She was assigned to Hofts for her last two years of graduate fellowship training in internal medicine. Since she was an internist and I was in the Surgery department, we didn't interact much. We crossed paths only a few times that first year, but my attraction to her was almost instantaneous. She was beautiful in a way that most female doctors doing their residencies and fellowships simply can't be – the long hours, the lack of sleep, and the bad food usually wreck your skin and make your hair fall out. But not Emma. The woman could work a thirty-six-hour shift straight through without sleeping and still come out looking like a runway model.

"I was smitten with Emma from the beginning, but I didn't have the opportunity to tell her so. Truth be told, I was terrified of her." Harlan stopped pacing for a moment, and stopped to catch his breath.

"About eight months after I met Emma, I called the attending physician in charge of Emma's fellowship program and asked if I could take her to lunch. I told him that I was starting a mentoring program between the Surgery department and the non-surgical specialties, which was complete bullshit, of course. But it got me an opportunity to talk to Emma alone, outside the hospital.

"Emma was an MD fellowship recipient only a year or so away from passing her final boards, not a green first-year resident. So it technically wasn't against regulations for us to date – even if it would be frowned upon. I thought I'd be all smooth and slick with Emma at the lunch, maybe even have her in my bed by dinner time. But boy, was I wrong. The woman was a force of nature. One look at her, I could barely even remember my name. She'd spent a year between med school and residency training in the Sudan working for Doctors Without Borders. I think she knew I had a crush on her, and used that to full advantage – by the end of our lunch, Emma had me hook, line, and sinker. I barely knew the woman, and in the space of thirty minutes, she'd managed to get me to agree to accompany her to the Sudan for her next three-month tour of duty, which would begin in no less than three weeks."

"Wow." Joanna was touched. "Emma really must have been something."

"You bet she was. Why the hell else do you think I went halfway around the world at the drop of a hat just to get a better chance of sleeping with her?"

Joanna wondered if Harlan would ever consider doing the same for her. She doubted it.

"I put in for a three-month leave of absence that very afternoon," Harlan went on. "The chief surgeon wasn't happy about losing me on such short notice, but the hospital administration was thrilled at the idea. Good publicity, and all that.

"I didn't get much chance to speak with Emma at all until the day before we were supposed to leave. She called me at home the night before our flight, offering to give me a ride to the airport. I wanted to ask her to dinner that night, but I clammed up completely when she called. I stayed clammed up the next day for the entire flight to Egypt. There are no commercial flights in or out of the Sudan, so Emma, me, and some of the other doctors assigned to our volunteer group made the crossing into the Sudan on armored Land Rovers. Emma and I shared the backseat of one of the Land Rovers for an eighteen-hour trip, and it was during that long, bumpy drive that I finally was able to loosen up around her. We ended up talking for almost the whole time.

"Within days, we were inseparable. We actually got married while we were in the Sudan. There was a Catholic priest in one of the refugee camps who married us. Neither of us were Catholic, but that didn't matter to us. That first tour of duty I spent there was the happiest time of my life."

Harlan sighed. A look of nostalgia mixed with regret began to build in his blue eyes; Joanna saw the lines around them deepen. At last, she was getting a glimpse of the source of this man's pain. Obviously something awful had happened to Emma, this woman he had loved so fully. But what?

"That first tour of duty was relatively calm, since there was a cease-fire in place. But there was still plenty of work for me to do. I treated mine victims, amputees, burn victims. Also lots of tropical diseases and cholera. But Emma was in her element the whole time. Treating and soothing the most desperate people on Earth – it was what Emma was born to do.

"The two of us returned to Hofts a married couple, not to mention minor celebrities. We raised a few eyebrows around the hospital with our quickie marriage, but that was about it. It was over and done with, and nobody tried to wave any stupid employee dating policies in our faces. Emma went back to finishing her fellowship, and I started publishing research based on some field surgery techniques I'd learned in the Army and then modified in the Sudan.

"That's when my research on infection control under the poorest of battlefield conditions got started. Along with publishing my research findings, I started developing inexpensive, contamination-proof field hospital supplies for use in developing countries – supplies that were cheap and easy for poor countries to produce and buy. I owned fifty percent of the patent royalties on everything I invented, with the other half going to Hofts. It made me a very, very wealthy man in more ways than one. For the first time ever, I had riches, I had love, and I had satisfaction in the work I was doing. And Emma was responsible for every bit of that."

"She certainly sounds like a wonderful person," Joanna sighed. "I've – enjoyed hearing about her. But I thought you were going to tell me about all the wrongs you've done. It doesn't sound to me like you've done any."

Harlan went back to pacing the room. "Emma and I had a few very good years together. We went on assignment with DWB together at least once a year. After two more tours in the Sudan, on our fourth tour, we were assigned to a new DWB project in Sierra Leone, another war-town, poor African country. The whole country was in chaos. Our refugee camp in Freetown was surrounded by soldiers and guerrillas who were always at each others' throats. Gunfire and bombs were commonplace just outside the fence.

"By the time we'd been in Freetown three months, the Revolutionary United Front had attacked our camp and hospital nine times. Time and again, our hospitals were raided, our medical supplies stolen. Many of the Westerners in other camps were captured and then held for ransom, if they were lucky enough not to be killed first. But Emma and I and all the other doctors, nurses, and aid workers in our camp were pretty much left alone. But after three months, the fighting around us intensified and things got a lot worse."

Joanna gasped. She knew what must have happened next. "Something happened to Emma there. Isn't that right?"

Harlan nodded. He stopped pacing and sat down beside her, leaned his head against her left breast. He cupped it gently into his left hand, squeezing and then stroking her taut nipple through the thin cotton of her scrub blouse. "Yes," he whispered. Joanna's breath caught in the back of her throat. She felt empathy for this man, deep empathy. Deep empathy, and deep attraction. Joanna found it harder and harder to resist the urges she felt tightening her stomach, melting her thighs, warming her heart at Harlan's touch. She had to help him, to comfort him, to ease his pain. And ease her own pain as well.

"Harlan, tell me what happened to Emma."

Harlan kept his face buried in Joanna's bosom for almost a full minute. Then he jerked away, and walked over to the two-story window. The first shadows of twilight were falling. As the sun began its final move towards setting behind the Blue Ridge horizon, Harlan spoke.

"Our tour of duty was almost over when it all went down. Things had gotten so bad we didn't dare leave the center of camp, not even for a few minutes. Some nights we both slept in the hospital tent rather than go back to our quarters, which were too close to the edge of camp for our liking when the skirmishes were close.

"Emma was pregnant. We'd just found out a week earlier, and both of us were ecstatic. But we were counting the days until we could get the hell out of Sierra Leone, too. The climate and the dangers of the camp wore hard on Emma, and she also had very bad morning sickness. I'd been working a double-shift in the clinic when Nihone, a local nurse who lived in our camp, burst into my office.

"Nihone broke the news that a pack of RUF mercenaries had just gotten into camp. They'd kidnapped several Westerners and refugees before they stole one of our Land Rovers and took off. One of the kidnapped Westerners was my wife. They'd taken her from our tent, where she'd been resting."

Joanna sucked in her breath. "Oh God, Harlan."

"Of course, then all hell broke loose. Those of us left behind tried to determine what would be the safest bet for retrieving our people. We decided based on the previous kidnappings of Westerners in and around Freetown that the best thing to do, at least for the first twenty-four hours, was wait for ransom notes. When the notes came, we'd probably be able to figure out where RUF was holding everyone and then do a rescue on the pretense of bringing ransom money. But twenty-four hours came and went, then forty-eight, and no ransom notes ever arrived. After three more days, somebody dumped all the bodies of the kidnapped outside our camp gate. Emma's body was there with them."

Tears spilled onto Joanna's cheeks. She couldn't imagine the pain, the grief, the horror that must torment Harlan's soul day and night.

"Joanna, It was my fault. I told Emma it was safe that night to sleep in our tent instead of at the hospital, and it wasn't. I failed her."

Joanna rushed over to Harlan and threw her arms around him. He collapsed against her into sobs. She stroked his hair, rocked him back and forth. "It's all right, Harlan. It wasn't your fault. You had no way of knowing—"

"It *was* my fault," he barked through his tears. "I slacked off. I didn't pay attention to how close the fighting had gotten. I knew better than to tell her to sleep alone in our tent. I failed her, Joanna. I failed the woman I loved."

"Hush," Joanna cooed, and rocked him back and forth some more. "Hush. I'm sure that wherever she is now, Emma knows you didn't fail her. She knows that you loved her. I know it, too."

Harlan broke away from Joanna's embrace and flopped back into one of the beanbag chairs. He covered his face in his hands for a moment, rubbing his closed eyelids. Then he looked up. "There's a lot more to this story. Failing Emma wasn't the only bad thing I've done."

He stood up and began to pace again. "Given what happened, Doctors Without Borders gave me permission to go back to the States three weeks early. When I got back to Boston I tried to pretend everything was back to normal, but I just went through the motions each day as if I were in a dream. The first year or so I pretended like my whole marriage to Emma had never happened rather than deal with the loss. That worked for a while."

"But it didn't last. A year or so after I returned to work, I started having problems. It was subtle at first. My attention span dropped.

It took me longer to concentrate, to focus. I lost my temper more easily, and more often. I became paranoid. I began accusing people of doing things that they of course weren't capable of doing. I even screamed at patients a couple of times.

"Some of my subordinates complained, but Hofts shrugged it off. I had an impeccable reputation, an excellent track record. Hofts didn't want to lose me, because my work attracted a lot of patients —and funding – to the hospital that it had come to rely on. Not to mention all the patent royalties I shared with Hofts on all my inventions – their share added up to several million dollars a year. I cruised through on that goodwill for another few years, but I was losing it, little by little.

"Pretty soon I started having anxiety attacks. I started drinking, taking Valium and other drugs I swiped from the hospital dispensary to take the edge off. Pretty soon, I was hooked. I was walking around on duty while high. There are days – whole weeks, even – that I don't remember because I was too stupefied on pills or booze.

"I started making mistakes. They were minor at first, but gradually it moved up to bigger things. Potentially dangerous things. I started mixing up my cases. I once left a sponge inside a patient. The nurse on duty caught that mistake before it could do any damage, luckily for me.

"That kind of thing started happening more and more often. My residents and nurses covered for me, first out of loyalty, then out of necessity – because Hofts was more than willing to put their employees and patients at risk in order to hang on to my millions of dollars' worth of patent royalties. To a point.

"Things escalated until there came a day late last year when I went in to surgery drunk and high off my ass. I could barely even walk, or so my most senior resident said. I don't remember going into the OR that day at all. Apparently my hands were shaking so much I couldn't even hold a scalpel, let alone operate on anybody. My senior resident and the head surgical nurse intervened, and called security to have me forcibly removed from the OR before the patient could be brought in. Administration was called. They sent me back to my townhouse near the Boston Common in a taxi. I woke up the next afternoon in my own bed at home, not knowing how I got there."

Harlan went over to the Sub Zero and pulled out another beer. After a moment, he shook his head and put it on the counter beside the sink. "Actually, I shouldn't be drinking. I shouldn't even have any of this stuff in the house. I really need to call my AA sponsor." He took the rest of the beers out of the fridge, popped them all open, and then dumped their entire contents in the sink. "I had a bad day today."

"You're an alcoholic," Joanna said, realizing.

"Among other things," Harlan chuckled. "An asshole, a pill-popper, a bad surgeon. If you want to leave now, I understand. I can drive you home after the beer has left my system, or I can call my housekeeper to come pick you up. Your choice."

"I—" Joanna couldn't speak. She needed to sit down, to think. Who was this man, really? Clearly, he was in a lot of pain. Joanna knew now that she loved Harlan Wilkinson. Of that she was sure. She knew that she couldn't confess that love – whatever kind of love it really was – aloud. Not now. Not yet. "I need some time, Harlan," she said. "Please."

He sighed. "I expected as much. At first I wasn't going to tell you all of this, because I figured it would just drive you away. But I can't be dishonest with someone I love, either. I love you, Joanna." Harlan's eyes pleaded for her to respond.

"I—" Joanna faltered. Then her mouth clapped shut. She couldn't say another word.

"You need some time," Harlan said.

Joanna nodded. She went to gather her things. Harlan's confession had hit her like a rolling boulder – yet, she completely understood why he'd wanted to keep the truth from her. "You can drive me home whenever you're feeling up to it," she finally heard herself say.

"All right. I understand completely. But there's one last piece to my story I still need to tell you."

Joanna steeled herself for the rest of the details, which surely would be awful. "Go ahead."

"After a certain point, Hofts had had enough of my drinking on the job. They let me go. After the drunken OR incident I agreed to enter a rehab program and to voluntarily have my medical license suspended for one year while I got cleaned up."

"I see," was all that Joanna could say. She finished tossing her things into her tote bag and turned her gaze back on Harlan. His eyes were brimming with tears; his lower lip quivered like so much jelly.

Harlan stared at Joanna with a look of longing that could span centuries. Joanna tried to look away, but his eyes followed hers wherever they darted. Every time his gaze met hers, Joanna felt a fluttering at the base of her stomach. He radiated love for her with every pore of his being; she felt its power rake over her, body and soul. His passion for her was a palpable, tangible thing – the pull from his watchful eyes was devastating, exciting, and soul-crushing all at the same time.

Her husband Bob had never looked at her like that.

Never.

Before she could take another breath, his mouth seized upon hers, sending her entire body into a vortex of sensation. Harlan's tongue traced the insides of her lips, raked itself over her teeth, and then plunged into the depths of her mouth until almost reaching the back of her throat. She kissed him back with equal force, exploring first his tongue and then the rest of his mouth, feeling, licking, tasting every molecule until she thirsted for more of him. She let her tongue trace the outside of his mouth, feeling the sharp little carpet of his razor stubble on his chin, then his cheeks. She buried her face into his neck, breathing kisses there until Harlan seized her by the shoulders and pushed her against the wall. His lips scorched a path down her neck that his tongue followed. He tore the collar of her thin cotton scrub blouse asunder, ripping the top portion of it until it hung askew, exposing her bra. He nudged the left strap off her shoulder with his nose, then traced a path of kisses to her nipple as her bra fell partially away. He rained kisses all around the edges of her breast, making her writhe in painful longing for him to seize upon the nipple that screamed for the liquid touch of his tongue. But instead of fulfilling that desire right away, he teased her, nibbling on the tender white skin that surrounded her breast's golden crown. The sensation of his lips, teeth, and tongue on the silken edges of her bosom was enough to make her beg.

"Please," she breathed. "Please."

Harlan raised his head to meet her eyes and ran the fingertips of his left hand across Joanna's swollen nipple, sending sensual shivers up and down her neck and spine. "Are we really going to do this, Joanna?"

"Take me, Harlan. I'm yours."

"Joanna—" He tore the rest of her blouse off her heaving body. He kissed the milky valley between her breasts, then licked a trail with his tongue downward towards elastic waist of her scrub trousers, which he flicked off her body with a quick jerk of his wrist. The scrub trousers were so loose that they slid right over her scuffed white nurse's shoes, which Joanna kicked off along with her socks as Harlan traced the lacy outline of her panties.

"You shouldn't wear those baggy scrubs so much, Joanna. A body this beautiful shouldn't be covered up." He eased her panties down slowly, caressing the inside of her thighs and the back of her calves as the silky fabric passed over them, making Joanna's breathing come in short, quick pulses. She lay there on the soft shag carpeting, naked save for half a bra cup that barely clung to her right breast, as Harlan stood over her, still fully clothed. The knowledge that she was in complete and total submission to this powerful, complicated man thrilled her in ways she never imagined.

"Please." Joanna found herself begging, wanting, *needing* more than she'd ever needed anything from any man, ever. "*Please*. Here. Now."

Joanna sat up and tore at Harlan's belt buckle, yanking his pants halfway down his legs until they caught on his prominent calf muscles. Joanna tore his boxers downward and pulled him to her. She arched her back, inviting him inside as a guttural cry escaped her throat. She closed her mouth over him in a liquid kiss. She relished the musky, metallic taste of him against her tongue, thrilled at the harsh sensation he made when he touched the back of her throat. She loved this man.

Harlan's climax was already close, very close. Seconds before he reached the point of no return, Harlan gently pushed Joanna off. "Take it easy, baby," he breathed. "Too much more of that, we'll be finished before we've even started." He stepped out of his sneakers and socks, then pulled off his pants, tossing them over his shoulder. His golf shirt stayed on; Joanna found that exciting, daring, and a little bit naughty all at once. He found a condom in his wallet and slipped it on. She parted her legs, expecting to receive him, but instead, Harlan fondled her intimately, first softly on the outside, and then suddenly, fiercely, on the inside. He searched for her pleasure points, and found all of them. Joanna writhed and thrashed under his skilled, ministering fingers as she came. And when she thought she could stand it no longer, Harlan slid right into her as if by instinct. The sheer heft and weight of him on and inside her was more than enough to make her come a second and a third time, and as she did, she called his name again and again and again.

They matched each other's rhythm perfectly, Harlan's hips sinking to meet her rising ones in thumping harmony. As their bodies rose and fell as one, Harlan's lips passed over nearly all of Joanna's torso, neck and arms – and with every kiss, he whispered delicate words of love to every pore, every inch of skin, every part and parcel of her. His ardor went from slow, soft, and gentle one moment to hard, fast, and urgent the next – and there were a hundred variations in between. Joanna's hands slid up and down Harlan's back, and as she rode higher and higher up a seemingly infinite mountain of pleasure, her fingernails sank deeper and deeper into his skin, finally drawing blood as he shuddered and groaned at the gush of his own orgasm. He collapsed against her, bathed in musky sweat that she tasted as she kissed his shoulder. It was a fast encounter, but it was a perfect one, too. Joanna and Harlan had achieved maximum pleasure in minimum time, and their love for each other was the reason.

They lay there in the afterglow for a long time, just enjoying the sound of one another's breathing. Joanna closed her eyes, relishing the last few tingles of pleasure as her body sank into a state of deep relaxation. Finally, Harlan spoke.

"Thank you so very, very much, Joanna."

"For what?"

"For this moment. For all of our time together – even the times when you called me an S.O.B. *Especially* those times, in fact."

"You're welcome," Joanna said, her voice so serene she barely recognized it as her own. "But I really don't know that I've done anything special."

"But you have. You're a very, very special woman, Joanna, and what you've done for me is even more special. Even if it all just ends here, you've given me everything I've ever wanted."

Joanna settled into the crook of Harlan's arm. Even as she basked in bliss, the creeping doubts that had plagued her ever since she first set eyes on Harlan plagued her yet again. What did he mean, *even if it all just ends here*? Did he think it would end? Did he *want* it to end? What happened next?

Joanna and Harlan fell asleep in each other's arms before either of them could give the matter another thought.

*****

Early the next morning, even before dawn began poking its fingers of light through the bedroom window, Joanna awakened to the smell of bacon and eggs. Harlan had left a clean Egyptian-cotton bathrobe for her on the edge of the bed, and had even set a new toothbrush and bar of Ivory soap, both still in their plastic wrappers, on the sink for her to use. Joanna was touched by these thoughtful gestures, which seemed so out of character for someone as publicly hard-edged and macho as Harlan.

After she'd had a chance to freshen up, Joanna descended the spiral staircase that led to the lodge's first floor. Harlan had a full breakfast set up on the kitchen table, complete with fresh-squeezed orange juice, tan cloth placemats, and matching cloth napkins in bamboo napkin holders. He set a plate of over-easy eggs and crisp bacon in front of her just as she sat down.

"I hope that's the way you like your eggs," he said, grinning. He was already dressed in jeans, a Hofts University sweatshirt, and a red-checked apron embroidered with *Real Men Cook*. "Since you're a stomach sleeper, I took a guess on over-easy."

Joanna smiled. The man was really too much. "You guessed right, actually. Except you forgot the Tabasco sauce."

"Hold that thought," Harlan said. He whirled back to the refrigerator, pulled out a half-empty bottle of Tabasco, and set it in front of her. "How's that?"

"Beautiful." Joanna smiled to herself. More and more, she was coming to realize that Harlan was the man she'd like to wake up to each and every morning.

"So, have you heard anything from the hospital?" she asked, savoring a bite of perfectly cooked egg.

Harlan's back stiffened slightly as he fried up his own batch of eggs. "No, I haven't. But I think I heard your cell phone ringing earlier. You might want to check for messages."

Joanna shrugged and went back to eating her breakfast. Retrieving voice mail messages was the furthest thing from her mind. Right now, all she wanted to do was bask in early-morning breakfast bliss with her new lover. Still, she was worried about the situation in Covington's surgery department. Never in her career had she worked any place that had been shut down by the state, and she was increasingly curious as to what was behind the sudden closing.

"I'm sure whatever it is, it can wait." She chuckled. "After all, our entire department's been shut down."

Harlan set down his own breakfast plate across from her with a clatter, and sat down across from her. "About that, Joanna. There's probably something you should know."

Joanna inhaled the impossibly fresh orange juice in one gulp. She figured Harlan must have gone to the store for it while she was still asleep – either that, or he had an orange tree stashed somewhere. "What?"

"*I'm* the reason the state shut Surgery down, Joanna."

Joanna set down her fork, and peered at Harlan, perplexed. "But why? Surely not because of your hand injury—"

Harlan held up his right hand. Joanna noticed that he'd removed the bandage since last night. The perfect butterfly stitches helping heal his torn palm were still there, but the cut was nearly closed over and the stitches could come out soon. "Joanna, just before I drove you here yesterday, Middleton called me to his office to tell me that I was under investigation by the state medical board. The surgery department will be shut down at least until my interim successor comes in next week."

Joanna blinked. "Interim *successor?* I thought they were just getting someone to fill in for you until your hand healed."

"Well, that was the original plan, until I got placed under investigation. Now I've been formally fired."

"Fired?" Joanna thought she might choke. "You mean, you've known this whole time, since before you brought me here yesterday, that you'd been fired?"

Harlan sighed. "I'm afraid so. That makes me unemployed, Joanna. I hope that doesn't make you fall out of love with me or anything." He gave her a look that was both sad and sarcastic.

"But why did they fire you?"

"Well, for showing such an interest in you, partially. When Middleton confronted me the *second* time on whether or not I was involved with you – just before you found me in the parking garage – I told him the truth."

Joanna got up from the table, put her hands to her temples. "Why would you tell me all those other – forgive me – *horrible* things about yourself all afternoon yesterday, and then leave out the one, tiny detail that you'd been fired as surgery chief just for—" Joanna's breath caught. "Just for wanting to be with *me?*"

"Well, in truth, Joanna, my involvement with you wasn't the only reason I was fired. The main reason was the state investigation, which if my calculations are correct, probably has something to do with the fact my medical license was suspended in Massachusetts while I was in alcohol recovery."

"Oh, no," Joanna said. "That's awful."

"Joanna, just chill out for a minute. This thing might not stick. When the truth comes back to Middleton about my Massachusetts license, I'm sure I'll be reinstated."

"When Middleton fires somebody, he means it, Harlan. After working at Covington as long as I have, I know that better than anyone."

Harlan scoffed. "I don't know why Middleton felt the need to jump the gun. The state investigators would have found, if Middleton had just given them the time, that I surrendered my Massachusetts license voluntarily. It was reinstated a year later without prejudice once I'd proven I was clean and sober. The fact is, I've had no problems with my surgery practice since then, except of course for the little cutting-my-hand problem at Covington – which, I might add, only happened because I was so damn attracted to you in the OR I could hardly see straight. Which really says something for how much Middleton values you and your nursing skills, considering Middleton gave up the hospital's entire cut of my patent royalties when he fired me."

"Wait a minute," Joanna said. The mention of Harlan's patent royalties piqued her interest. Suddenly her ex-husband Bob's mysterious accusations in her parking lot a few days ago made more sense. Bob had always had a talent for sniffing out easy money – and then spending it just as fast. He must have found some way to get at those patent royalties, and Joanna was willing to bet he'd offered somebody a cut of the profits if they helped him. "You say that the hospital lost its cut of its patent royalties when they fired you? Are you sure?"

Harlan nodded. "It's in my contract. Unless there's some legal loophole I missed out on, Joe Middleton threw away millions of dollars when he fired me."

Joanna immediately fished her cell phone out of her purse. Sure enough, her caller ID showed a number of calls – two from Bob, two from Bob's sleazy attorney, and to Joanna's shock, one from her own divorce attorney. "Do you have a copy of your contract?" she asked.

"Yeah, upstairs in my study." Harlan looked bewildered. "Why?"

"Go get it," Joanna ordered. "Then come with me. We need to pay a visit to my lawyer."

Chapter Twenty-seven

JOANNA AND Harlan sat in the well-upholstered office of Peter Landall, Joanna's divorce lawyer. In addition to handling her divorce from Bob, Peter and his firm had been Joanna's family lawyer for three generations, handling her grandparents' and parents' real estate transactions, their wills, even a traffic ticket or two. There was no one she trusted better to help her and Harlan understand the strange goings-on with Covington Community Hospital's administration – not to mention what her ex-husband Bob might have to do with it.

Peter Landall – who between his white seersucker suit, gold pocket watch, and slow drawl was the epitome of the Southern country lawyer stereotype – finished poring over a pile of files, polished his wire-rimmed spectacles, and spoke. "Joanna, I knew it was only a matter of time before you showed up in my office. That ex-husband of yours is up to no good."

"I know that," she replied. "That's why I divorced him."

Peter opened a desk drawer and took out a binder, which he opened. "Well, I think this goes a bit beyond his usual shenanigans," he said. "By any chance has Bob's sleazy lawyer Rod Slokowski been calling you lately?"

"Yes," Joanna said. "He's left me at least a dozen threatening messages over the past few days. I've ignored them all."

Peter sighed. "Well, Joanna, you aren't going to be able to ignore him anymore. You see, Mr. Slokowski had filed suit against you on Bob's behalf. Here's the brief."

He passed it across the desk for her to read, but Joanna couldn't make heads or tails of the legalese. "What does this mean?" she asked.

Peter templed his fingers underneath his chin and sighed. "Bob has got it into his head that you cheated him out of millions of dollars in your divorce settlement just because you've taken up with Dr. Wilkinson here. Of course, you weren't involved with Dr. Wilkinson until well after you and Bob divorced, so that's pretty groundless as far as I'm concerned. But it seems that Bob's managed to convince some pretty high-up people at the hospital to testify that the two of you had an adulterous affair while you and Bob were still married."

"But we weren't!" Joanna cried. "I didn't even meet Harlan until three weeks after my divorce was final!"

"I know, Joanna." Peter sighed again and shook his head. "But based on these two testifying witnesses, the divorce court has agreed to re-examine the settlement order. I'm not sure how Bob and his lawyer have managed to get these witnesses to out-and-out lie for them, but my guess is it's got something to do with money. Lots of it. Like a cut of your patent royalties, Harlan."

Harlan looked puzzled. "But didn't Joe Middleton throw away the hospital's cut when he fired me?"

Peter shook his head. "Not in this case," he said. "There's a loophole buried in the fine print he's taking advantage of. Or, at least he *thinks* he's taking advantage of, anyway. The hearing's been scheduled for tomorrow morning. I've been through the documents in question and I think I can find a way to nip this in the bud. But I'll need the both of you to work with me in the office this afternoon to plan our strategy. Think you both can do that?"

Joanna and Harlan exchanged glances, and nodded.

*****

Before the hearing the next morning, Peter Landall waited for Harlan and Joanna at the top of the courthouse steps. He refreshed their memories of what they'd discussed in his office the day before, and coached them on what kind of testimony he'd be expected to give, what questions the opposition might ask. "I think if all goes our way, this unpleasantness will be behind us shortly," Peter drawled, rocking back and forth on the balls of his feet while he thumbed his suspenders.

But Joanna didn't share Peter's optimism. After all, she knew the low depths her ex-husband was capable of sinking too well. And the fact that he longtime hospital superiors and colleagues were in cahoots with him made her ill.

Joanna took a long, deep breath in a vain effort to regain her composure. Her head felt light and her palms were sweating gallons. She swallowed hard despite the huge lump forming in her throat, and finally ascended the courthouse steps, clutching Harlan's hand.

*****

"ALL RISE!" shouted the bailiff, a heavyset, middle-aged woman with a voice as deep and rich as most men's. "Court is now in session! The Honorable Judge David J. Diviston presiding." Judge Diviston, the very same white-haired man who had publicly proclaimed three months earlier that Robert and Joanna Watson were divorced, strode into the courtroom, his black silken robes flowing. Following Peter's gentle gesture, Joanna took her place in the defendant's box, while Bob and the ever-sleazy Rod Slokowski (in one of his trademark silver-sharkskin suits) took their position in the petitioner's box. Just as Joanna had predicted, Joseph Middleton sat behind them on one of the witnesses' benches. And to Joanna's shock, Shirley Daniels sat right beside him, looking smug.

Judge Diviston settled into his heavy mahogany chair on the judge's dais, shuffled some papers from a file, and looked up. He glanced from Bob to Joanna and then back to Bob again. "Well. Mr. and Mrs. Watson. You're back."

Rod Slokowski stepped forward, grease practically oozing from every pore on his slick, bloated face. "Your Honor, my client wishes to obtain a new divorce settlement on the grounds that Mrs. Joanna Watson not only hid financial assets from the court, but also committed adultery."

Judge Diviston adjusted his bifocals and sighed. "Yes, I read the brief, Counselor. Mrs. Watson's counsel has submitted a written denial of both allegations, so you'll need to provide a corroborating witness."

"We have two corroborating witnesses, Your Honor. Divorce petitioner respectfully calls Joseph Middleton to the stand."

The portly old man Joanna had worked under for so long lumbered up to the witness box. Joanna ground her teeth at the betrayal.

Rod Slokowski rubbed his hands together like a slumlord and approached the witness box. "Mr. Middleton, would you care to describe a conversation you had with Dr. Harlan Wilkinson on Tuesday of this week?"

"Yes," the old man replied, with much effort. "I called Dr. Wilkinson into my office to respond to some reports I'd had of him improperly cavorting with a nurse." There was a tremor in his voice, and he couldn't look Joanna in the eye no matter how hard she stared him down. Did Middleton really *want* to be testifying against her? He certainly didn't look like he was too happy about it. Joanna wondered if the old man might have been coerced.

"And what nurse was Dr. Wilkinson allegedly cavorting with, Mr. Middleton?"

"Ahhhhm, Joanna Watson."

"The woman standing just over there?" Slokowski gestured towards Joanna. Middleton nodded, never once meeting Joanna's eyes. "And what did Dr. Wilkinson say about these allegations when you confronted him?"

Middleton coughed. "Well, ahhh, the first time I spoke to him about it, he denied everything. But the second time, he ahhhm, he admitted it. That's all."

"And you fired Dr. Wilkinson after he made that admission, did you not?"

Middleton's lips pursed and his brow furrowed. He gave a slight nod, but did not answer verbally.

Slokowski seemed a bit put off, as if Middleton hadn't given him the exact answer he should have. But after a split second, the slea- zy lawyer regained his slick courtroom composure. "Let the record show the witness nodded in the affirmative. And is it also correct, Mr. Middleton, that your subordinate Shirley Daniels informed you that Mrs. Watson and Dr. Wilkinson had been engaged in an affair for several months – perhaps years – dating back to a time before Dr. Wilkinson moved to Statesville? An accusation corroborated by my client?"

Peter Landall stood. "Objection, Your Honor. This is hearsay."

The judge sighed again. "Sustained. Mr. Slokowski, do you have any other evidence to present besides hearsay? And when I say evi- dence, I mean photographs, videos, audio recordings, et cetera, that would show Ms. Watson committed adultery? If you don't, I'm not even going to entertain the hidden-asset allegation."

Slokowski cringed. "No, Your Honor. But I could possibly have more evidence tomorrow, if you'll grant a recess—"

"Denied," the judge barked, and banged his gavel. "Will there be any rebuttal from Ms. Watson's side?" the judge asked. "Not that you need to given how flimsy the case is."

"Yes, Your Honor, there will," Peter Landall drawled, and bowed to the judge as gracefully as Robert E. Lee at Appomattox. "As you've already read in our own petition, Your Honor, Ms. Watson formally denies the allegation of adultery and wishes the divorce settlement to stand under the previously agreed-upon terms."

"Duly noted, Counselor," the judge muttered, fiddling with his pen. He wore the look of someone who would rather be fishing or hunting – anything other than presiding over this petty hearing. "Do you have a witness or witnesses present to rebut the petition- er's, ahhh, allegation?"

"We do, Your Honor. We respectfully call Dr. Harlan Wilkinson, to the stand."

Rod Slokowski, Bob, and Middleton collectively did a double-take. Shirley Daniels went several shades of green. Clearly, Peter Landall had not notified opposing counsel of the witness list. Harlan strutted up to the stand and sat down. Peter Landall approached the witness box, keeping his manicured hands clasped behind his back. "Sir, please state your name," he drawled.

"Harlan Wilkinson, MD."

"You are a physician, are you not?"

"Yes," Harlan said. "People with 'MD' after their names generally are, you know." Joanna recognized that voice. It was the gruff, rude, off-the-cuff voice he'd first used with her in the Covington Community Hospital elevator weeks ago. It was the voice that had made her simultaneously detest and desire him. His *I'm-a-world-famous-surgeon-so-don't-you-fuck-with-me* voice.

Mr. Personality was back.

Unruffled, Peter never once let go of his gracious Old South manners. He paced back in forth in front of the witness box as if gliding on air. "Of course, Dr. Wilkinson. You are quite well known in your field, are you not?"

"Oh, sure. In surgery circles, I'm world-famous. And rich, too."

Peter stopped pacing. "Just how rich are you, Dr. Wilkinson?"

Rod Slokowski stood up. "Your Honor, I object."

Judge Diviston set down his pen and sighed for the umpteenth time. "Overruled, Counselor. After all, you brought this case to court in an attempt to show your client had the right to Dr. Wilkinson's money. The witness may answer the question."

Harlan smiled. His azure eyes pierced Joanna's jade ones as he replied, "I am worth approximately eighty-seven million dollars, give or take, according to my last tax return."

A collective gasp rose from the courtroom. Joanna froze. She'd known Harlan was wealthy – but not quite *that* wealthy. She felt all the blood drain from her face and settle pleasantly into the space between her legs.

Peter didn't even blink. Clearly, he'd been prepared for Harlan's answer. "Eighty-*seven* million dollars, you say? Very nice, Dr. Wilkinson. Now we all know that even the most successful of surgeons don't generally earn that kind of money just by taking out appendixes. Would you care to tell the court what the major source of your income is?"

"Certainly. Patent royalties. I invented numerous medical devices and tools which are now successfully sold worldwide by companies like Johnson & Johnson, Tyco, Medtronic, and others, chiefly to Third World countries. I still own a share of all the patents, and get a royalty payment for each and every one of my devices that are sold. And millions upon millions of my devices have been sold. I think you can do the math."

Peter Landall started to pace again, never once unclasping his hands from behind his back. "You said you only own a *share* of your patents. Who owns the other share, or shares?"

"Well, Hofts University, my former employer, used to own a share, but they forfeited it when they fired me for my alcoholism. A problem I overcame with proper treatment, I might add." Harlan glanced up at the judge, who nodded his approval. "Another share goes to a charitable foundation based in Boston. When I signed my chief of surgery contract with Covington, the hospital assumed the share that Hofts gave up when they fired me."

Peter Landall rocked back and forth on the balls of his feet. "Thank you for that explanation, Dr. Wilkinson. Now, when Mr. Middleton terminated your employment at Covington Community Hospital for allegedly cavorting with Ms. Watson against hospital regulations, you assumed that, per the terms of your contract, Covington would forfeit its share in those patent royalties upon your firing, is that correct?"

"That was my assumption, yes."

"I see." Peter walked to the counselor's table and pulled a document from his briefcase. "I have a copy of your contract here. Dr. Wilkinson, next time you sign a contract such as this one," he said, indicating the document, "I suggest you read the fine print. Would you care to read the clause I have highlighted?" Peter handed Harlan the document. Harlan took it, squinted at the highlighted passage, and read it aloud.

"The terms of the aforedescribed Patent Royalties Share shall be deemed Forfeit In Whole and Full to the Employer, Covington Community Hospital, in the event that the Employed, Harlan Wilkinson, MD, shall ever have his medical Licensure Revoked and/or be placed under investigation by the State Medical Board of North Carolina while under the Employer's Employ."

Realizing the meaning of what he had just read, Harlan's forehead began to show beads of sweat.

"Thank you for reading that, Doctor," Peter chirped, taking the document back from him. "And isn't it true, Dr. Wilkinson, that at the time Mr. Middleton dismissed you from service, you had just been suspended from active call duty by the hospital as a result of a pending investigation by the State Medical Board of North Carolina?"

Harlan's jaw tightened, and he shot a look of sheer fury straight at Middleton, who reddened. "That is correct."

"Thank you, Dr. Wilkinson." Peter Landall grinned in triumph. "Your Honor, I think it is clear based on both Mr. Middleton's and Dr. Wilkinson's own testimony, as well as the supporting documentation provided in the brief I submitted on behalf of Ms. Watson, that the true motivations behind today's court petition are actually part of a sinister and fraudulent scheme on the part of Mr. Watson, his attorney, and their two witnesses to share in the patent royalty rights Mr. Middleton and his hospital have wrongfully tried to wrest from Dr. Wilkinson."

Joanna silently thanked her now-deceased parents for teaching her to always trust Peter Landall and his law firm.

"Your Honor, I submit that Mr. Watson's allegations are nothing more than a slander meant to embellish and advance his counsel's and others' illicit scheme," Peter went on. "I further submit that the nature of these actions should not only cause Mr. Watson's petition be dismissed, but also that Mr. Slokowski's and Mr. Middleton's – and by cooperation and association, Mr. Watson's and Ms. Daniels's – actions be referred by Your Honor to the appropriate authorities for investigation on federal racketeering charges. I also have submitted a copy of my brief to the State Medical Society of North Carolina requesting that their investigation of Dr. Wilkinson be aborted, as it was likely initiated by Mr. Slokowski for questionable causes. I also have requested the hospital board consider removing Mr. Middleton from administering Covington Community Hospital, and also to reinstate Dr. Wilkinson to staff as soon as possible." Peter folded his arms across his chest, waiting for the judge's response.

Judge Diviston looked from Peter over to Slokowski – who by now had turned several shades of purple – and snickered. "Mr. Landall, it's always a pleasure having your grace and decorum in my courtroom. Lawyers like Mr. Slokowski could learn a lot from you. Mr. Watson, your petition is dismissed. Unless there is any further business on this case, this court stands adjourned. Happy divorce, folks."

Judge Diviston banged his gavel. Bob Watson, Slokowski, and Middleton all bolted from the courtroom as if the soles of their feet were on fire, but Joanna, Peter, Harlan, and the few citizens who'd been sitting in the gallery remained. The judge gathered his papers and moved to get up from his seat when Harlan stepped up from the witness box and approached the bench.

"Your Honor, I have business before this court."

"Dr. Wilkinson, if you plan to sue Mr. Middleton and Mr. Slokowski for slander, libel, and attempted theft of patent rights —which I strongly suggest you do – you'll need to do that in a federal court," the judge said. "I don't preside over that sort of thing. I'm a family court judge." The grizzled old jurist started to leave. But Harlan blocked his path, alarming the bailiff.

Leave it to Harlan to try and strong-arm a judge, Joanna thought, stifling a chuckle.

"I'm aware of the law in those matters, sir, and I plan to pursue it in the appropriate court," Harlan said. "But as a family court judge, in addition to granting divorces, you can also perform marriages, isn't that correct?" Harlan glanced over at Joanna, who jerked up from her chair when she saw the look on his face. As he gazed upon her, his badass-surgeon persona melted away in favor of a look of pure, majestic love and adoration. "Because you see, Your Honor, I love Joanna Watson, and I'd like to marry her as soon as possible. Today, preferably."

Judge Diviston smiled. "Well now. That's a horse of a different color."

Harlan crossed the courtroom to Joanna's side and took both her hands in his. She saw that he'd had the stitches removed from the right one, which was now perfectly healed. "Your Honor, I assure you that my intentions towards Ms. Watson have always been honorable. I want to marry her, be the father of her children, work with her, live with her, and grow old with her. That is, if she'll have me." Harlan went down upon one knee, gazed up at Joanna, his eyes brimming with tears. "Joanna, I love you. Will you marry me? Here? Now? Please?"

Joanna couldn't move. She couldn't speak. She couldn't even breathe. Her thighs were jelly, her lower belly tomato soup. She wanted to say yes – *needed* to say yes – but for some reason she couldn't get her mouth to form the word.

Judge Diviston placed a firm hand on her shoulder. "Ma'am, I suggest you hang on to this here fellow. I'm willing to bet my law degree he's the most lovestruck puppy in all of North Carolina."

The judge's strong grasp was enough to unstick Joanna's lips. "Y-yes, Harlan," she stammered. "I'll marry you. Right here, right now. No conditions. Just my love."

They embraced for a long time; then Harlan's mouth seized upon hers, and they kissed with more wanton abandon than any courtroom should ever have witness to.

THE END